Big Trouble Ahead!

"But our football game is for fun," I said. "Like— you know how sometimes rock stars play a big softball game to benefit a charity? It's that kind of thing."

But Kiri didn't seem to hear me. She just bulldozed on. "I will not run a story to promote your game, Tara. And we don't take ads for sexist events."

At last Cassie found her voice. "But the powderpuff game *is* school news!" she blurted out. "As editor of the school paper, it's your job to write about it!"

Kiri was quiet for a minute. Then she said, "You know, I think I should write about your game. Yes. I will *definitely* write about it."

"Well . . . great!" I said.

"Check the editorial column this Thursday," she advised. "You'll see plenty about your game." Kiri's smile looked anything but friendly.

The Paxton Cheerleaders

Go For It, Patti!
Three Cheers For You, Cassie!
Winning Isn't Everything, Lauren!
We Did It, Tara!

Available from MINSTREL Books

THE PAXTON CHEERLEADERS™

We Did It, Tara!

Katy Hall

A Parachute Press Book

A MINSTREL® BOOK

PUBLISHED BY POCKET BOOKS

New York   London   Toronto   Sydney   Tokyo   Singapore

This book is a work of fiction. Names, characters, places, and incidents are products of the author's imagination or are used fictiously. Any resemblance to actual events or locales or persons, living or dead, is entirely coincidental.

A MINSTREL PAPERBACK *Original*

A Minstrel Book published by
POCKET BOOKS, a division of Simon & Schuster Inc.
1230 Avenue of the Americas, New York, NY 10020

ISBN: 0-671-89787-X

First Minstrel Books printing February 1995

10 9 8 7 6 5 4 3 2 1

PAXTON CHEERLEADERS is a trademark of Parachute Press, Inc.

A MINSTREL BOOK and colophon are registered trademarks of Simon & Schuster Inc.

Cover art by Aleta Jenks

Printed in the U.S.A.

for Joe
from Urgent Computer Care,
Ronkonkoma, New York

CHAPTER 1

*B*ORING!" I exclaimed.

I stretched out on a grass-green couch in our living room and admired my newly polished toenails—which were blue. My three best friends—Cassie Copeland, Lauren Armstrong, and Patti Richardson—were at my apartment for a Friday night sleepover. Just then, they were all staring at me.

"Why, Tara?" said Cassie. She sat across from me on another couch. I couldn't quite decide if her pale skin and her wild red hair clashed with the green of the couch fabric or not. As usual, Cassie was scribbling in her precious notebook. I swear, everything in her *life* is written down in that little black book! "Why not a bake sale?" Cassie asked me.

"It's *boring!*" I repeated. "And besides, we'd have to bake a zillion cookies to earn enough money for our whole cheerleading squad to go to the clinic. Plus," I added, "germs."

"Germs?" Cassie's eyebrows went up.

"Yeah. You know how when you bake, you lick your fingers and then stick them back in the batter?"

"Gross!" Cassie tossed a pillow at me. "I don't!"

"Everybody does," I said, catching the pillow and popping it under my head. "I *never* buy stuff at bake sales."

Cassie drew a line through *bake sale* in her notebook. "Beth Ann said that if we want to reserve a spot for our squad at the clinic," she went on, "we have to send in a thousand-dollar deposit by December first. That gives us a little more than three weeks to raise the money."

Beth Ann Sorel is our cheerleading coach. She'd asked all of us on the squad to brainstorm moneymaking ideas this weekend. She knew how much we wanted to go to that clinic.

"All the really good squads in Indiana will be there over spring break," Lauren added. She sat beside Cassie in a nest of yellow and pink pillows, which brought out the richness in her dark brown skin. "Paxton Junior High has *got* to be there, too!"

Patti brushed a wisp of blond hair off her forehead. I thought the purple pillow behind her made her blue eyes look even bluer. "Maybe we shouldn't have used up our whole budget going to the state cheerleading competition," she said.

"Are you serious?" Cassie cried. "We took third in that competition! It put Paxton on the map! And that's another reason we have to go to the clinic."

Patti frowned. "What do you mean?"

"We have to see the stunts the first- and second-

2

place squads are doing," Cassie told us. "And learn to do them *better!*"

"Cassie!" I exclaimed. "We don't have to win everything."

"Why shouldn't we?" Cassie asked. "We're good enough."

"It's sick to be so competitive," I grumbled. "Don't you ever do anything just for fun?"

"Winning at the competition *was* fun," Cassie declared.

"I wish I'd been there!" exclaimed Lauren.

Lauren had been so psyched to go to the competition. But a friend from her old gymnastics team, Danielle Alverez, really needed some extra coaching. And Lauren was the only one who could do it. Lauren had to choose between coaching Danielle and going to the competition—and she chose to help her friend.

"How about a car wash?" Patti suggested. "My cheerleading squad in Dallas used to raise *tons* of money washing cars."

"It's not as boring as a bake sale," I agreed. "But by the time we organized it, it'd be the middle of November . . ."

"And we'd freeze," Cassie finished for me.

"What about a raffle?" said Lauren. "We could raffle off . . . I don't know . . . a bike? Rollerblades?"

Cassie frowned down at a page of figures in her notebook. "We *might* make a thousand dollars on a raffle. But why not think of a way to pay for the *whole* clinic? Let's see. It's one hundred fifty dollars for each cheerleader. Multiply that times eighteen girls on our squad,

3

and you get twenty-seven hundred dollars." She looked up at me. "Plus another hundred and fifty dollars for you as our alternate, Tara."

"For one brief happy moment," I said, trying to sound tragic as possible, "I'd forgotten that I'm only the lowly alternate!"

I wasn't really used to being alternate. Not long after football season started this fall, Kelsey McGee, another seventh grader on the squad, broke her ankle. I'd taken her place as a cheerleader for almost two months. But now Kelsey's ankle was fine. And now I was back on the sidelines.

Cassie rolled her eyes and kept on talking. "And that's not counting money for transportation or meals or anything." She sighed. "We need to make at least three thousand dollars."

Patti whistled. "That sure is a lot of money," she said.

"But if anybody can think of a way to make it," Lauren said, "it's us!"

Now Cassie sprang up from the couch. She stuck out her arm, with the palm of her hand facing down. "Let's hear it for the four of us!" she said. We all jumped up and slapped our hands on top of hers. Then she lowered her hand and popped it up, sending all of our hands into the air.

The four of us became "the four of us" last August. That's when we all showed up at the cheerleading clinic for seventh graders trying out for the PJHS squad.

The minute I saw Patti there, I knew she'd make cheerleader. She brings new meaning to the word

4

peppy. Her toe-touch jump is totally awesome. And boy, can she raise some school spirit!

Lauren's been my friend since kindergarten. I knew she'd make the squad, too. She was a national gymnastics champion. But she traded her balance beam for a pair of pom-pons. At the end of one of our cheers, she does six back handsprings in a row! Let me tell you, *that* gets a crowd cheering!

Cassie's super serious about the *leader* part of cheerleader. She wants to run for President of the USA one day! She says getting a crowd to cheer with you is great leadership experience.

But when I walked into the gym the first morning of that clinic, lots of girls couldn't believe their eyes! Even Lauren was shocked. "Tara! *You?*" she said. "At a cheerleading clinic?"

Everybody was so surprised because I'm not what people think of when they think "cheerleader." I'm tall and not very athletic—although when it comes to dancing, look out! I'm awesome when there's music on! And maybe it's not easy to picture me in a cheerleading uniform, either. My clothes are definitely way outrageous! But—hey! I'm a cheerleader. Get used to it! Really—there's no such thing as a cheerleader type anymore.

I went to the clinic last summer because of a magazine article my mom showed me. It told about a college that has a great theater program. Mom knows I plan to be an actor some day. She also knows I'm going to need a scholarship. She and my dad got a divorce when

I was two, and she doesn't take any money from him. Anyway, this college gives scholarships to cheerleaders.

I can make up pretty good songs. So I figured I could make up good cheers, too. And I have a loud, deep voice that carries for miles. I thought cheerleading sounded like a piece of cake. *Wrong!* I wouldn't even be an alternate if I hadn't been put into a practice group at clinic with Patti, Cassie, and Lauren. No way!

What happened was this. Patti had just moved to Paxton from Dallas, where she'd been a cheerleader since she was four years old. Amazing, huh? She showed up at the clinic dressed totally in the Paxton colors—a little yellow shirt, a blue cheering skirt, and a blue baseball cap. Almost everybody else had on cutoff jeans and T-shirts, so Patti stood out.

Naturally, I stood out, too. I wouldn't be caught dead in drab old cutoffs! I remember what I wore that first day of clinic: a yellow tank top and royal blue spandex bike pants, with blue scrunch socks and my black-and-white zebra-print sneakers.

When Patti started talking, her Texas accent *really* made her stand out. One of the girls at the clinic, Darcy Lewis, began making fun of her. That burned me up and I let Darcy know it.

I guess Patti was grateful to me for rescuing her from Darcy. When she saw that my toe-touch jump wasn't the greatest and that I couldn't even come close to doing the splits, she invited me—and Cassie and Lauren—over to her house after the clinic ended to practice for tryouts. Patti's mom had been co-captain of the University of Texas cheerleaders. (The other co-captain was her own twin sister!) For two solid weeks Mrs. Richardson coached us in a mirrored room in their house that used to be a dance studio. Patti's little sister, Missy, calls it "the cartwheel room."

But just when things were going great, Cassie got bossy. She insisted that we had to start practice at eight-thirty every morning. Well, I am *not* a morning person. Most days I showed up around ten. Cassie was furious. She kept nagging me and nagging me. Finally I stomped out of that cartwheel room and ran home. I'd had it with Cassie and her schedules *and* with cheerleading!

Later that day Cassie, Patti, and Lauren showed up at my front door. Cassie apologized and begged me to keep practicing. Lauren told me how important it was to her that all four of us make the squad together. So I moved in with Patti for a few days. Mrs. Richardson and her twin sister, who was visiting from Dallas, worked with me then. And I mean *worked!* They didn't let me rest for a minute. Even when I sat down to take a break, they made me stretch. But it all paid off! I'm a Paxton cheerleader—even if I am only the alternate, as Cassie had just pointed out.

Now I flopped back down on the couch and looked at my watch. "Only fifteen minutes until 'Model Mania' comes on," I said. "Ooooh, what will Veronica be wearing this week? And I can't wait to find out who pushed Samantha off the yacht! I'm betting on Geoffrey."

"No TV until we've thought of a way to raise three-thousand dollars," Cassie declared, folding her arms across her chest.

"Get real," I told her. "This program is my life!" I was only exaggerating slightly. "Model Mania" had the worst actors, the worst dialogue, and the absolutely *worst* fashions imaginable. It was a total hoot!

But I knew the only way to get Cassie to back off was to come up with an idea. So I closed my eyes and started thinking. My mind flipped through every money-raising idea I'd ever heard of, short of bank robbery. Just before ten o'clock I sprang up from the couch. "I've got it!" I yelled.

"What?" Cassie said. "What? What? What?"

"You said no TV until we'd thought of an idea," I told her as I picked up the cartons from the pizza we'd had for supper. "Well, I've got one," I added as Patti helped me fold out the couches into queen-size beds. "But I'm not telling what it is until *after* 'Model Mania'!"

CHAPTER
2

eoffrey! You never pushed Samantha into the shark-infested waters that night! You're covering for somebody. I know you are!"

"Veronica! Where is your brain?" I shouted at the TV as the program faded out at the end. "Can't you see he's soooo guilty?"

"Show's over!" exclaimed Cassie, sitting bolt upright. "Time to tell your idea, Tara."

"After the previews," I protested.

Cassie hit the Off button. "Now," she said.

"I can't believe you did that!" I wailed. "Now I have to wait a whole week to see Veronica's next outfit!"

Cassie just stared at me. She's an only child, and her parents are both extremely serious musicians. At her house they *never* watch sitcoms or soaps. Sometimes I think that's what's wrong with Cassie. She has no appreciation of the fun of *junk*.

"Okay, here goes," I said. "A fashion show! The cheerleaders can be models. The stores at the mall can lend us clothes. We could even dress like the characters from 'Models Mania'!" I looked from Lauren to Patti to Cassie. "It's fantastic, right?"

"Wrong!" said Cassie. "For starters, we'd lose half our paying customers because boys wouldn't come to a fashion show."

"They might." I wasn't giving up so easily.

Cassie just shook her head. "Wait!" she said suddenly. "How about a quiz show? Like 'Jeopardy'! We could get contestants from every grade. And the teachers could make up the questions."

"Oh, great!" I said. "It sounds just like school!"

For a moment no one suggested anything else.

"Well," said Lauren at last, "we could have a talent show."

"You could do your balance beam routine!" Patti suggested.

"Yeah!" Cassie agreed. "We could charge a tryout fee for contestants, and an acceptance fee for the acts, and—"

"This sounds too complicated," Patti put in. "Anyway, we're cheerleaders. Shouldn't we do something . . . cheerleaderish?"

"You're right!" Lauren agreed. "Like something to celebrate the football season. Something for the last game."

"Football with a twist," I said, thinking out loud. "Hey, what if the seventh- and eighth-grade cheerleaders challenged the ninth-grade cheerleaders to a football game?"

"All-girl football!" exclaimed Lauren. "All right!"

10

"We could challenge them in the school paper," I added. "Or on a poster, where everybody in the school would see it. Then we'd sell tickets to the game."

"You mean *us?*" Cassie's eyes were wide. "Play football?"

"Sure!" exclaimed Patti. "In Texas we called them 'powder-puff' games." She giggled. "They were real popular."

"Powder puff! I love it!" I said, laughing. "And maybe we could get the guys on the football team to be our cheerleaders!"

"You think they'd do it?" Lauren asked.

"Sure," I told her. "We're always cheering for them. It seems to me like they owe us a little cheering."

Lauren grinned. "Tara, can you see T.D. cheering?"

T.D. Yeager was a tall, blond seventh grader on the football team. I had an on-and-off crush on him. This week it was *off.*

"T.D. shaking pom-pons!" added Patti, cracking up.

"I'll ask him when I see him in math class on Monday," I said. "I bet he'll do it and talk the other guys into it, too."

Cassie broke into a smile. "We can sell hundreds of tickets!" she said. "We'll make a bundle! We'll fill the football stadium. We can sell popcorn and hot dogs and T-shirts and—"

"Hold it," I said. "You know, some of the other girls on the squad might come up with another moneymaking idea."

"Maybe," Cassie admitted. "But I just know ours is better."

I heard keys jingling then, and a second later my mom walked into the apartment. She was carrying a white take-out bag from the deli down the street, and she looked pretty tired.

"Hello, girls," Mom said as she took off her coat and headed for the kitchen.

My mom's a hairstylist at Sabrina's Salon. Most nights she doesn't get off work until ten. Sabrina does her own advertising on the radio. In a voice that's totally hoarse from a lifetime of smoking cigarettes, she says, "Ladies, visit Sabrina's Salon, the nighttime beauty spot for today's working woman." I can imitate Sabrina *perfectly*. It always cracks up my mom and her friend, Eva, who's the manicurist at the salon.

Mom sat down on a high stool at the kitchen counter and kicked off her shoes. She took an egg salad sandwich and a can of tomato juice out of the bag. I went over and sat down on a stool beside her. I didn't want her to feel like she was eating alone.

"So, how are you girls tonight?" Mom asked. "You got something to eat, didn't you?" she asked before taking a bite.

"Pizza from Gino's," Lauren told her.

"It was really good, Mrs. Miller," Patti added. "Thank you."

"Any time," Mom said. "I love it when you girls sleep over here. It reminds me of my old slumber party days. We used to scare ourselves silly watching horror movies on 'The Late Show.' "

"Right! Mom was always telling me about this really creepy movie called *Invasion of the Body Snatchers*," I said, putting an arm around Mom's shoulder. "So we rented the video one night, and it was about as scary as 'Sesame Street'!"

"It *was* scary, Tara," Mom protested. "When people went to sleep, aliens turned them into pod people with no emotions."

"Ooooooh, big-time scary, Mom!" I teased her.

"Mrs. Miller?" Cassie said. "This isn't scary or anything, but listen to what we came up with tonight." And she told Mom all about the powder-puff football game. She told about organizing ticket sales and selling hot dogs. It sort of sounded like she'd thought it all up. It's not like I wanted any big credit for the powder-puff idea or anything. But at the same time I didn't want bossy little Cassie to step in and take it over, either.

"But," Mom said, "do you girls know how to play football?"

"I do!" Patti said. "My dad made sure of that!" Patti's father used to be quarterback for the Dallas Cowboys!

"Me, too," Lauren added. "I've spent my life playing touch football with my big brother and his friends."

"I don't," said Cassie.

"That's okay," I said. "I don't, either. The whole thing's just for laughs. The worse we are, the funnier it'll be!"

Mom smiled and shook her head. "You can count me in for two tickets. I'll bring Eva—she'll get a kick out of it."

Eva's divorced, like Mom. But she doesn't have any kids. Eva and Mom do just about everything together.

I really like Eva, but sometimes I wish Mom would go out on a date!

"What should we charge for tickets?" Lauren was asking.

"Let me think for a second," Cassie said, and she flipped through the pages of her notebook. "Six hundred kids in the junior high," she muttered, "plus eight hundred in the high school makes fourteen hundred, so if we—"

"Five dollars," I said quickly. "Five dollars a ticket."

"Isn't that sort of a lot?" asked Lauren.

"Yeah," said Patti. "In Dallas tickets were a dollar."

"Well, in Paxton tickets to a powder-puff game are *five* dollars," I said. "And worth every penny."

Cassie snapped her notebook shut. "Sounds good," she said.

I grinned. It felt great to be making decisions. It felt great to have Cassie agree with them. For once, I was in charge!

CHAPTER
3

*B*ORING! I thought as I listened to my math teacher. Ms. Brickman was talking on and on and on about x, the unknown quantity. It was Monday afternoon, and math was my last class of the day. And if x wanted to be an unknown quantity, that was okay with me.

T.D. Yeager sat in the desk in front of me. Even the back of his neck was a whole lot more interesting than x. T.D. had light blue eyes and light, almost white, hair. His skin, at least the skin I could see on the back of his neck, was just about as pale as the sheet of notebook paper I was doodling on.

"Tara?" Ms. Brickman said suddenly.

I looked up. "Yes?"

"Have you found what number x represents?" she asked me.

"Mmmm, no, not quite," I confessed. I began twisting a piece of fringe on my black leather vest. I'd picked up the vest at a thrift shop. It had silver studs all down the front, and it looked fabulous with my black, lace-up combat boots.

"Well, why don't you come up to the board? Let me see how you'd go about finding it," Ms. Brickman said.

I looked at the problem on the board. It was full of numbers with lines under them and parentheses and multiplication and division signs—not to mention my old friend x. I didn't have a clue what to do.

"Oh, Ms. Brickman, have mercy!" I begged. "If I come up there to do that problem, I'll just get the whole class confused!"

Lots of kids started giggling when I said that.

But Ms. Brickman looked as stern as ever. "All right, Tara," she said. "I'll let you sit this one out. But please see me before you leave today."

"Okay," I said. Then I kept my eyes glued to the board as Annie Goff went up there and turned mixed numbers into fractions, multiplied numerators, got rid of parentheses, and finally wrote the answer to the big mystery: $x = 3$.

Three? That was it? Boy, it sure seemed like a lot of work to end up with a measly little number three!

After class I gathered my books together.

"Are you watching football practice today?" T.D. asked me.

If cheerleading practice ends early, I like to sit in the bleachers and watch the boys go through their plays. Partly—I'll admit it!—I like watching boys. And partly I like learning more about football. My dad's a major football fan. But he lives in Chicago with his new family. It's just an hour by train from Paxton, but still, I don't get to spend that much time with him. So I have to pick up my football tips where I can.

"I'll try," I told T.D., shouldering my backpack. "Listen," I whispered, "you know how our squad is trying to raise money so we can go to the big cheerleading clinic over spring break?"

"No," said T.D.

"Well, we are. And—keep this a secret, because it's not for sure yet—we're thinking about having a powder-puff football game."

"A *what?*" T.D. asked.

"The seventh- and eighth-grade cheerleaders are challenging the ninth-grade cheerleaders to a football game," I whispered.

T.D. frowned. "There aren't enough cheerleaders to make two teams of eleven."

"It doesn't matter," I told him. "It's not supposed to be a serious game. It'll be hilarious. Especially if some of you guys on the football team would be cheerleaders for us!"

T.D. just stared at me. "What do you mean, exactly?"

"You know. Wave pom-pons and do cheers for us."

T.D. narrowed his light blue eyes.

"Come on!" I urged him. "We cheer for you guys every Friday! It's the least you can do for us!"

"Yeah, all right," he said. "It might be fun. But no way am I wearing a cheerleading skirt."

"Did I say anything about a skirt?" I asked innocently. We could discuss the fashions later!

"Tara?" Ms. Brickman called from her desk.

"I'll be right there, Ms. Brickman," I called. Then I turned back to T.D. "Ask Drew and some of the guys on the team if they'll do it. Talk them into it, okay?"

T.D. rolled his eyes. "Good luck with the Brick," he said.

I grinned as I watched T.D. head for the door. This powder-puff game was going to be *huge!*

I trudged to the front of the room. "Thanks for not making me come up to the board, Ms. Brickman," I said.

"Next time I won't let you off so easily," she warned. She slipped her pencil behind her ear, which was hidden by a smooth dark blond helmet of hair. "Working with a student at the board gives me a chance to see where any problems are," she said.

"With me, they're *everywhere,*" I joked.

Naturally, Ms. Brickman didn't smile. Instead, she opened her grade book and put a ruler under my name. Silently I read across the scores that came after it: 82, 75, 71, 64.

"I haven't entered your latest score," Ms. Brickman said, pushing the test paper toward me. In red ink she'd written 57%.

"Uh-oh," I breathed. I'd really studied for that test, too. At least I'd started to. But everybody was counting on me to make up an original cheer for the cheerleading competition. Plus one for the kids at Memorial Hospital—and math got left behind.

"You're a bright student, Tara," Ms. Brickman said. "But in my class you're going steadily down hill." She tapped on her calculator. "Your average *with* your latest test score can be rounded up to 70—that's just barely a C minus."

I nodded.

"If your next score is lower than 70, your average will go down to a D. This is serious."

"It is," I agreed. "I'll get suspended from cheerleading if any of my grades go below a C."

Hearing this seemed to brighten Ms. Brickman up a bit. "Well," she said, "maybe that will motivate you to work harder."

"It will," I told her. "For sure."

"You know I have extra-help sessions three mornings week," she added. "Tuesday, Wednesday, and Thursday at seven forty-five. I'd like to see you in here tomorrow, Tara."

"Okay, Ms. Brickman," I said, groaning on the inside. "I'll be here."

I left her classroom, heading for cheerleading practice. I thought how much trouble I had getting out of bed on a regular morning—on a morning when I had a *great* day ahead of me. How would I ever, *ever* make myself get up to come to an extra math class?

CHAPTER
4

I quickly changed into my practice clothes—a black sweatshirt, hot pink bike pants, orange socks, and bright white cheering sneakers. Then I hurried into the gym. Short, blond Beth Ann Sorel had already changed out of whatever she wore to teach ninth-grade history. Now she stood under a basketball hoop wearing blue sweats and, as always, her blue Paxton baseball cap. She'd already started our meeting. Quickly I dived for a spot on a mat between Patti and Lauren and began stretching.

"We want to do the new 'Lions Fans!' cheer for the Riverview game," Susan Delgado was saying. She was our ninth-grade squad captain. She had dark eyes and always wore her sleek dark hair in a ponytail. "It ends with three flyers up in extension stands. I think that's what we should work on today. Plus our dance numbers."

Beth Ann nodded. "Thanks, Susan," she said. "Okay, let's talk about fund-raising ideas. Did any of you girls come up with anything over the weekend?"

I looked over at Lauren, Patti, and then Cassie. We'd agreed that I'd bring up our idea when I thought the time was right.

"We did!" Michelle Bostick called out. Michelle was small and had short blond hair. She ran against Cassie for seventh-grade co-captain and beat her. Cassie had never lost an election before in her life. When she found out that I'd voted for Michelle because I thought she'd make a better co-captain, Cassie went nuts. But later she forgave me. She even admitted that her scheme to try to buy votes was *not* a good idea!

Whenever Michelle said "we," she meant herself and her best friend, Deesha Taylor. Deesha is as tall as I am—five feet seven—and has deep brown skin. Lately, she's taken up weight training and boy—is she ever developing some biceps!

"We could sponsor a Rollerblade race!" Deesha said.

"Count me out," Kelsey McGee muttered from behind me. "I'm not breaking my ankle again!"

"We'd charge people an entry fee," Michelle was explaining. "And there'd be a big prize for the winner."

"Sounds interesting," Beth Ann said. "Any other ideas?"

Sara Feld, the eighth-grade co-captain raised her hand. "How about an auction?" she said. "We could go around to stores and ask them to donate things that we could auction off."

"Another good suggestion," said Beth Ann. "Any more?"

"We could have a marathon dance contest," said Heather Smyth, a ninth grader. "Everybody would get

21

people to pay like ten dollars for them to dance ten minutes or something."

"I did the AIDS Dance-a-thon last year," Susan Delgado said. "It was really cool and raised a ton of money."

"But this year's AIDS dance is coming up," said Andrea White, another ninth grader. "We don't want to compete with it."

"I've got a *great* idea," said Christina O'Connor, a tall, blond eighth grader. "We could have a big bake sale!"

Now seemed like the *perfect* time to bring up an original idea! With a quick look at Patti, I raised my hand.

"Here's something to end the football season with a bang," I said. "The seventh- and eighth-grade cheerleaders could challenge the ninth-grade cheerleaders to a *huge* football game!"

"Football?" said Sara Feld. "Are you serious?"

"Totally," I said. "We can make the challenge so that the whole school knows about it. Then we'll sell tickets to the game. Patti says in Dallas they call them 'powder-puff games,'" and I added in my best Texas accent, "and they're real, real popular!"

Everybody laughed—especially Patti!

"That does sound like a fun way to raise money!" exclaimed Susan. Lots of other girls were nodding and whispering excitedly.

"Hold it," said Christina. "What if we've never even tossed around a football?"

"All the better for us!" exclaimed Isabel Greenburg, a ninth grader.

"Right!" said Andrea. "We'll beat you guys by fifty points!"

"No way!" called Deesha.

"But I don't want to get tackled!" Christina whined.

"Don't worry!" I assured her. "The whole thing is done as a joke. It's not serious football. And," I added, "maybe the guys on the football team could be our cheerleaders!"

Everybody cracked up at that idea.

"I could coach them," offered Steve Liu, our trainer. "I can show them how to do some easy stunts that are pretty impressive."

Steve had been a cheerleader at Paxton High. Now he studied physical therapy at a junior college. I think he's majorly good looking. I always tell Cassie how I hope I'll get injured so that Steve can give me first aid. It drives her crazy!

"Well, that's certainly an interesting idea," Beth Ann was saying. "Okay, anything else?" When no one offered any more ideas, she said, "All right, let's vote."

Powder puff won by a landslide!

"The ninth graders will slaughter you lowly seventh and eighth graders!" called out Heather.

The rest of the ninth graders chimed in. Everybody was getting into the spirit of the game. It made me feel great!

"Anything else, Tara?" asked Beth Ann.

I'd been thinking about this ever since the sleepover on Friday night. I was ready!

"We need a publicity committee to make a big splash

23

with the challenge," I said. "And to make advertising posters. Any volunteers for publicity?"

Patti, Deesha, and Cassie raised their hands.

"You got it!" I said.

"Tara?" said Jane Underhill, one of the ninth graders. "Go talk to Kiri Kelly—she's the editor of *Pax News*. Maybe she'll do a feature story on the game for the school paper."

"Okay," I said. "Now, who wants to make ticket books?"

Two ninth graders volunteered.

"And who wants to sell tickets?"

Lauren and Michelle said they did.

"And we need somebody to ask the guys on the football team if they'll lend us some old football uniforms, and if maybe we could borrow their shoulder pads and things."

Susan and another ninth grader, Joannie Nichols, volunteered to do that.

And so it went until everybody on the squad had a job—except for Cassie, who had several.

"I think that does it," I told Beth Ann, and I sat down.

"Thanks, Tara," said Beth Ann. "That took plenty of organizing on your part. I'm impressed."

"Nah, it was nothing," I protested. But inside I felt great! For once, I was really running the show!

"All right, cheerleaders," Beth Ann said, clapping her hands. "Warm up. Then get into your groups. I want to see some dynamite extensions! And then let's

24

go through the two new dance numbers we've been working on."

After practice I talked Cassie, Lauren, and Patti into coming out to the football field with me.

"Maybe Drew will be out there," I said to Patti, and her face started turning pink.

Drew Kelly lives next door to Patti. He wears little round glasses and isn't very big. He doesn't look much like what you think of when you think *football player.* But he can run like anything, and he's the star quarterback of the PJHS team!

Drew's a big fan of Patti's father. (And, in my opinion, of Patti!) He's always finding excuses to come over to Patti's house—like he's looking for his dog. Right! Anyway, Patti says she isn't interested in him—and that he isn't interested in her. But whenever she hears his name, she goes into a major blush.

Patti, Cassie, Lauren, and I walked around the side of the school. We sat down on the bleachers just as football practice ended. I waved to T.D. He waved back. In a couple of minutes he and Drew walked over and sat down on the bleachers with us.

Another boy on the team, Justin Dubow, came with them. Justin looks *exactly* like what you think of when you think *football player.* He's *huge.* I mean, the guy has four chins! He can look scary, but he's really nice, and sort of shy.

"So I told the guys how you want us to be cheerleaders," T.D. informed me.

"So?" I said.

25

"So some of the guys said they'd do it." T.D. grinned.

"Hey! That's great!" exclaimed Lauren.

"Not me," Justin muttered.

"Aw, come on, Jus!" I coaxed him. "You'd be great!"

Justin shook his head, looking sort of sick to his stomach.

"Steve Liu said he'd coach you guys," Cassie told T.D. "He said he'd show you how to do a few easy stunts."

"Doesn't he think we're up to the hard stuff?" asked T.D.

"No!" I told him, laughing. "You guys will probably be as awful at cheerleading as we are at football."

CHAPTER 5

*C*an you see those guys trying a pyramid?" Lauren said with a laugh. Lauren, Patti, Cassie, and I huddled together as we walked home so we could talk over the wind. At five o'clock it was almost dark.

The four of us almost always walked home together after practice. Lauren and I live in downtown Paxton. Cassie lives way west of town in fancy-schmancy Paxton Heights. But she always meets her father in town at the radio station, WBMG. Mr. Copeland has his own classical music program called "Mozart in the Morning." Cassie does her homework at the station. Then her dad drives her home to Copeland Castle—which is what I call their big stone house. Patti lives in a subdivision just east of school. But she usually walks home with one of us, and her mom picks her up later.

"I think it's cool that the guys are so behind us on the powder-puff game," I said.

"Patti and I want to do some sketches for the advertising posters tonight," Cassie said. "We're thinking of

27

drawing a girl in a football uniform with powder puffs for pom-pons."

"If," Patti added, "we can draw the powder puffs so they don't just look like regular old pom-pons."

"Tara and I are going to work on the challenge posters," Lauren said. "Right, Tar?"

"Right, Laur," I answered. "But first we are going to torture ourselves by doing our algebra homework."

"I did my math homework during class today," Cassie said. "So I can definitely do some art for the powder-puff game."

"Cassie," said Lauren, "you're in eighth-grade math! How can you whip through the homework like that? Isn't it hard?"

"Not for me," Cassie said. "Mother told me that lots of musicians are naturally gifted in math. She and my father both are. So, even though I'm not that musical, I guess I inherited the math part."

"I *love* music!" I said. "But it sure doesn't do anything for my math grades!"

"I love math," Cassie said. "It always makes sense."

"Not to me," I muttered. "Anyway, for the newspaper ad," I added quickly to change the subject, "I was thinking that if there's time to get something into this Thursday's paper, we could do a mystery ad."

"Ads aren't supposed to be mysteries," Cassie objected. "They're supposed to *sell* something!"

"But we could say something like 'The Powder Puffs Are Coming!' " I went on. "Everybody would wonder what it meant. Then the next week we could run an ad that explained it."

"But there isn't time to stretch it out like that," Cassie said. "We've got to let everybody know about the game as soon as we can. We have to start selling tickets!"

"It *would* sell tickets," I said through clenched teeth as we reached my apartment building. "Oh, never mind. 'Bye, guys!" I said to Cassie and Patti.

"See you tomorrow!" Lauren called to them.

Then Lauren and I walked under the tall iron gate that surrounded Lakeview Apartments. Our building is three stories high, and our apartment is on the top floor. Mom says that when she and I first moved in, we really could see Lake Paxton from the bedroom windows. But now lots of taller buildings have gone up between us and the lake. So, good-bye lake view!

Lauren and I walked around the swimming pool, which was covered for the winter, through the court-yard, and up two flights of steps along the outside of the back building. Then, as I've done ever since my mom started working at Sabrina's four years ago, I knocked on the door of Apartment 3-A.

"Hi, Mrs. Huey," I said when our frail seventy-year-old next-door neighbor opened the door. "I'm home."

"Hi, Mrs. Huey," echoed Lauren.

"All right, Tara," Mrs. Huey said. "You girls call me if you need anything, will you?"

"We will. You do the same," I said. Then, as always, Mrs. Huey watched as I pulled out the long thin silver chain I wore around my neck. On the end of the chain was my apartment key. After I unlocked our front door, I waved to Mrs. Huey. Then Lauren and I went into our apartment.

In the winter when it gets dark early, Mom always leaves one of the living-room lamps on for me. While I turned on more lights, Lauren phoned her grandmother to say she'd be home around seven. Then she turned the radio to Z101. Luckily, Mrs. Huey doesn't hear too well, so the loud music doesn't bother her a bit.

"I'm going into the pit to see your gerbils," Lauren called as she opened the door to my bedroom. "Kirstie!" she called. "Lillie! How are you, babies?"

Lauren gave me the gerbils last year. Her gerbils have had so many babies that practically all the kids at our grade school ended up with one or two of them.

The pit is what I call my room. It's pretty big, but it has the world's teeniest closet. With my wardrobe this is a major problem. So I've just sort of let my clothes and shoes and scarves and stuff flow out of my closet into the rest of my room. I'm not exactly an organization freak, but I know which piles of clothes on my floor are ready to wear. And which ones are ready for the wash. Over my bed I have this great old stuffed moose head. I got it at a yard sale for only ten dollars! I call him Macauley, and I use his antlers for a hat rack.

While Lauren talked baby talk to the gerbils, I danced myself into the kitchen. Boogeying in time to the music, I grabbed two raspberry yogurts, a box of chewy granola bars, and a big bottle of mango-peach juice. Then I bopped into the living room and set our snack down on the coffee table. I put the cordless phone within easy reach and tossed half the pillows over to Lauren's couch.

"Okay," I said when Lauren came out of my room. "Now we are ready to hit the books!"

As I opened the big swamp-green algebra textbook, teensy numbers and letters and xs started swimming before my eyes. I slammed it shut. "Hey, Laur?" I said. "If I tell you something, you swear you won't tell?"

"Cross my heart, Tar," Lauren said, just the way we had promised each other since kindergarten.

"Especially Cassie," I said. "I'd die if Cassie knew this."

Lauren crossed her heart again.

"I'm having a major math emergency," I said.

"Uh-oh," said Lauren.

"Big-time uh-oh," I told her. "You know what I got on the last test? A fifty-seven!"

"Oh, Tara!" Lauren said, looking worried.

"The Brick said I still have some kind of C minus, minus, minus average," I said. "But if I don't do better on the next test, I'll go down to a D! And you know what that means."

"You'd be suspended from the squad," she whispered.

I nodded. "I can't let that happen," I said. "I just *can't!*"

"It won't," Lauren said. "You can pull out of this."

"But I'm totally lost about what's going on in algebra," I wailed. "When I look at those problems, all I think is, *Huh?*"

"I'll help you," Lauren said, picking up her math

31

book and coming over to sit next to me on the couch. "Let's just work on math. Somebody else can make the challenge posters."

"I already wrote something for them," I said. Then I dug around in my backpack until I found a crinkled sheet of notebook paper. "Maybe you and Patti and Cassie could do the lettering," I said, handing the paper to Patti.

"Definitely," said Lauren. Then, for the next two hours, she talked me through my math.

"Okay, I get it!" I'd shout as she finished explaining a problem. "I really and truly get it!"

Then I'd try to do the next problem by myself. And I'd get all mixed up again.

When Lauren said she had to go home, I flopped back on the couch, groaning. "I think my mom dropped me on my head when I was a baby!" I said.

"She did not!" said Lauren. "What are you talking about?"

"That's the only explanation for me and math," I told her. "The algebra portion of my brain was destroyed!"

Lauren laughed. Then she grew serious. "Math's not easy for me, either, you know."

"But you get it."

"I've put in plenty of hours with this baby," she said, thumping the ghastly green textbook.

"Yuck. How can you stand it?"

"I think about my cats," she said. "And my gerbils and my lizards. And how I really, *really* want to be a vet someday."

32

"And you need good math grades for vet school,"
I said.

"Yep," said Lauren. "So, that sort of keeps me going
when I'd rather quit."

"Yeah?" I thought for a minute. "Maybe I'll try
thinking about my favorite cheers. Maybe that'll keep
me going. That and Ms. Brickman's early-morning help
sessions tomorrow."

"We just can't hide that Lion pride!" Lauren chanted
from one of our cheers as she put on her coat.

She walked out the door then and I chanted after
her: *"Lions rule! We are cool!"*

CHAPTER 6

*H*i, sweetie!" Mom yelled over the music as she came into the apartment a little after ten that night. "I've got your favorites," she added, holding up a large white take-out bag from the corner Chinese restaurant. "Moo shu veggies and spareribs! Can you turn that music down a notch?"

"Sorry," I said. I heaved my body up from the couch where I'd kept working on math for *hours*. I hit the radio off. Then I walked into the kitchen and poured myself another glass of mango-peach juice. Mom poured herself a small glass of white wine.

"How was work?" I asked her.

"Fantastic!" Mom took two plates out of a cabinet and set them on the counter. "My last customer was so thrilled with the fabulous highlighting job I did that she gave me a big fat tip." She grinned. "So, we feast tonight."

"Three cheers for tips!" I said. "So, what went on today?"

Mom loved telling me about work. And I loved hearing her stories. It's *never* boring at Sabrina's Salon! Just last week a woman brought her cocker spaniel in for a perm!

Mom and I are really close. I guess because we've been just the two of us for so long. We look a lot alike. We both have thick, straight brown hair and blue eyes. We're both tall, and close enough to the same size so that we can share clothes. We both love to paw through the bins at thrift shops to find great old outfits at great low prices. Sometimes I think we're more like sisters than a mom and a daughter.

We're also—as Mom says—"creatures of the night." We hate to go to bed, and we hate to get up early. Mom's even worse than I am when it comes to getting up. So I get myself up, grab a fast breakfast, and walk to school. I don't mind.

"Sabrina hasn't had a cigarette for three days," Mom was saying. "I think she's really quitting this time."

"I hope so," I said. "Smoking is *nasty!*"

Mom put two super-thin pancakes on our plates and began spooning the vegetable mixture into them.

"How was school?" she asked when we were sitting side by side at the counter.

"Awful," I moaned. Then I told her about my latest math crisis, and how Lauren had tried to help. "Plus I'm going to Ms. Brickman's help session tomorrow morning," I added.

"That's the way, sweetie," Mom said. "I know you can catch on to this math if you'll tune in."

I'd just finished gnawing on a sparerib when the phone rang.

"I'll get it," I said, sliding off my stool. I knew it was my dad. He always calls between ten and eleven to make weekend plans. He knows Mom will be home then to okay them.

"Paxton Auto Repair," I said when I picked up the receiver. "You scratch 'em, we patch 'em."

Dad sells cars. We always try out car jokes on each other.

"Ha-ha, Tara," Dad said. "I thought I had a wrong number."

I walked the phone into the pit for some privacy. Mom and Dad don't speak to each other. Not directly. Just through me. And although Mom's never said this, I don't think she likes to overhear me talking to my dad. I'm not sure why my parents got divorced. Once I overheard Mom telling Eva something about "how Joe wasn't dependable." But I don't know. Maybe they were just too young to make it work. Anyway, as they've both told me a million times, it had nothing to do with me. After the divorce Mom refused to take any money from Dad—not even money for me. I think that's cool. Mom says this way she's totally independent.

After we chatted about this and that for a while, Dad said, "So, you're coming to see us this weekend, aren't you?"

When Dad said *us,* he meant himself, his wife, Diane, and their baby, Lucy.

Dad was already engaged to Diane when he introduced me to her. I was in fourth grade then. Diane was young and peppy and pretty, with her strawberry-blond hair and freckles. I liked her right away. She asked me to be in the wedding, along with her younger sister, Taffy, who's just four years older than I am. The wedding was great. Taffy and I wore long green velvet bridesmaids' dresses with baby's breath flowers in our hair. It's not my usual style, but everybody said I looked pretty fabulous in that dress.

After Dad got married, I couldn't *wait* to go to Chicago on the weekends. Diane would take me shopping and buy me the wildest earrings! When my Dad told me that he and Diane were going to have a baby, I was so excited. I loved helping them paint the baby's room and fix it all up.

Then Lucy was born. Boy, was she one cranky little bald-headed baby! My dad and Diane didn't seem to notice, though. Dad bought a video camera and spent every spare minute pointing it at the baby. He and Diane called her their "wittle bittle oochie coochie pie!" Could that make you sick, or what? Now Lucy's two. She still gets cranky sometimes. But mostly she's pretty cute.

"I'm coming," I told Dad. "How about if I take the eleven o'clock train on Saturday?" As I said this, I stuck my head out my bedroom door. Mom nodded that this time was fine.

But Dad was quiet for a minute. "We were hoping you'd be able to come on Friday afternoon," he said at last.

37

"Our football games are on Friday afternoons," I told him for at least the hundredth time.

"Well, are you cheering this Friday?" Dad asked. "I thought you only cheered if somebody got sick or injured."

"That's right," I said stiffly. "But I have to stick around—just in case somebody starts barfing on the field or something."

Dad sighed. Then he said, "Well, how about coming right after the game? Diane and I have a party to go to on Friday night, and you know you're Lucy's favorite sitter."

Now I love my little half sister, Lucy. What I didn't love was Dad and Diane using me as a baby-sitting service!

"Well, why don't you go to another party on Saturday night," I said, loading my voice with sarcasm. "I'll sit for Lucy then. But I can't come Friday afternoon."

"I understand," Dad said softly.

That's when I started feeling like a really horrible awful person. This year it seemed as if there was always something going on in Paxton that I just *couldn't* miss—football games and dinner at Bingo's with all the other cheerleaders and sleepovers with my friends. I even hated missing trips to the Paxton Mall!

"You know we just want to have you with us as much as we can, Tara," Dad was saying. "If the eleven o'clock train on Saturday is the one you want to take, then we'll be at the station at twelve to meet you."

"No, that's okay, Dad. I'll come Friday after the game," I told him. "I'll take the six o'clock train."

38

"Great!" Dad sounded really happy. I hoped it was mostly because he wanted to see me and not just because he wanted me to baby-sit!

"Kiss Lucy for me," I said. "Diane, too. See you!"

When I crawled into my bed that night, I set my alarm for—gulp!—six-thirty. Then I tried to go to sleep really fast. But of course I couldn't.

I stared at the ceiling, remembering. When I was a little girl, Dad would come to pick me up for the weekend in his incredibly cool 1956 red Chevy convertible. Then, with the top down and our hair flying, he'd drive along the back roads from Paxton to Chicago. On the way we always stopped at Debbie's Diner and ordered chocolate sundaes and talked.

I missed those times with Dad. Just before I drifted off to sleep, a thought popped into my head: Maybe sometimes Dad missed them, too.

CHAPTER 7

*T*uesday was not my day. I overslept. I missed the math help session. I also missed part of my first-period class. I'd rushed around like crazy getting dressed, and I felt totally un-together—like maybe I had something on backward or something. Tuesday felt like a bad hair day for my whole body.

But during lunch period I made myself go to the *Pax News* office anyway. Getting an article about our game into the paper was more important than how I felt. Cassie came with me.

"Hi," I said to a boy wearing a gray plaid flannel shirt. He was sitting at a desk near the door of the *Pax News* office, staring at a computer. "Is Kiri Kelly here?"

"Uh-huh," he answered. His eyes never left the screen. I thought his name was Brad Benton. And that he was a seventh grader.

"Could we talk to her?" I asked.

"I guess," he said, nodding his head in the direction of a closed door. "But she's pretty busy."

"We'll be fast," I said, and I headed for the door.

"Wait!" Cassie whispered when we were almost there. "If she's busy, let's come back."

"But when?" I asked.

"I don't know. Tomorrow, maybe?"

"But if we want something about the powder-puff game in this Thursday's paper, we have to talk to her today," I pointed out.

Cassie looked sort of nervous. "Kiri practically runs this school," she said. "I'm sure she's got a million things to do. Maybe we shouldn't bother her."

"But this is important!" I exclaimed. "What's the matter? You act like you're scared to go in there or something."

"I am not!" Cassie snapped.

Cassie's nervousness was making me nervous. But I knocked on Kiri's office door anyway. I thought I heard a faint "Come in," so we walked into the room.

Most of it was taken up by a big old wooden desk, covered with neat stacks of papers. Behind the desk, holding a phone to her ear, sat the ninth-grade editor of *Pax News,* Kiri Kelly.

Kiri had a slender face, a turned-up nose, and large brown eyes. Her straight light-brown hair was held back from her face by a plastic tortoiseshell headband. Okay, I could accept the headband. And maybe even her gold chain necklace and matching bracelet watch. But the gray wool suit jacket with large gold buttons? Unacceptable!

Kiri held up a finger, as if telling us she'd be right with us. "What you're suggesting is censorship," she

41

was saying into the phone. Her voice was deep and sort of husky. "We're not changing a word of that article. No, it's running the way it is."

Kiri hung up then. She slipped a yellow pad out of a large, overstuffed bag by the side of her chair and jotted down something on it. Then she looked over at us. "Yes?" she said.

Cassie opened her mouth. But nothing came out.

So what could I do? I started talking.

"I'm Tara Miller," I began, "and this is Cassie Copeland. We're cheerleaders, and our squad is trying to raise money to go to this big cheerleading clinic over spring break, and we need to raise three-thousand dollars."

The pleasant expression on Kiri's face changed to a slight frown.

"Anyway," I kept going, "the seventh- and eighth-grade cheerleaders have challenged the ninth graders on the squad to a powder-puff football game and—"

"To a *what?*" Kiri exclaimed.

"To an all-girl football game," I explained. "They're called powder-puff games. They're not real games. They're done for laughs—you know."

"No, I *don't* know," Kiri said. "Let me get this straight. To raise money, the cheerleaders are going to play football?"

I nodded.

"Even though you'll play so badly you'll look like idiots?"

"Uh, when you describe it like that," I said, "it doesn't sound right. But that's basically it, I guess. And

42

the guys on the football team are going to cheer for us," I added quickly.

"They're really behind us," Cassie squeaked in a high voice.

"We thought you might want to do a story on the game," I said, getting to the point at last. "We'd like to run an ad for it, too."

Kiri pressed her lips together. "Do you know how retro your thinking is?" she asked at last.

"Excuse me?" I said.

"Retro," Kiri repeated. "It's short for retrograde. Old-fashioned, behind the times."

"What?" I couldn't believe what I was hearing!

But Kiri just kept going. "The fact that you tried out for cheerleading in the first place means you haven't got a clue about feminist thinking!" Kiri's eyes darted from me to Cassie and back again. "But the idea that you are willing to play a brutal game invented by males to act out their need to dominate other males—*that* is unforgivable!"

"But it's for *fun!*" I said. "Like—you know how sometimes rock stars play a big softball game to benefit a charity? It's that kind of thing."

But Kiri didn't seem to hear me. She just bulldozed on. "I will *not* run a story to promote your game. And we don't take ads for sexist events."

At last Cassie found her voice. "But the powder-puff game is school news!" she blurted out. "As editor of the school paper, it's your *job* to write about it!"

Kiri was quiet for a minute. Then she said, "You

43

know, I think I should write about your game. Yes. I will *definitely* write about it."

"Well ... great!" I said.

"Check the editorial column this Thursday," she advised. "You'll see plenty about your game." Kiri's smile looked anything but friendly. "This could turn out to be a great opportunity."

"What's that supposed to mean?" I asked her.

"An opportunity for the whole school to get a little lesson in feminist thinking," she said. "And after my editorial comes out, you know who's going to show up at your powder-puff game?"

"Who?" Cassie and I asked together.

"Nobody!" Kiri said. "That's who!"

CHAPTER 8

You think she'll do it?" Cassie asked me as we scurried down the hallway. We were trying to make it to our classes on time. "You think Kiri will write an editorial against our game?"

"Oh, who cares," I answered. "Nobody reads the editorial stuff in the school paper anyway."

"I do," said Cassie. "But maybe she won't really write it."

"Trust me. Nobody will pay any attention to it," I said. "Besides, Kiri's not as smart as everybody thinks she is."

Cassie's eyes widened. "Yes, she is. She has the highest grade-point average in the whole school. She's president of the National Honor Society! How can you say that?"

"Because," I said, "nobody with a working brain could pick out the clothes she was wearing. Did you see those *buttons?*"

The sixth-period bell started ringing then. Cassie and I dashed to our classrooms before it stopped.

* * *

"Joannie and I went to Stone's Sporting Goods yesterday," Susan Delgado reported to start off our cheerleading meeting that afternoon. "The football players didn't have enough extra uniforms for us to borrow. We told the Stones about our powder-puff football game to raise money so we could go to the clinic, and Mrs. Stone said they'd *donate* football jerseys!"

"All right!" several girls called out.

"Naturally, they'll say 'Stone's Sporting Goods' on the back," Susan finished up. "But that's cool."

"What color are they?" Deesha asked.

"Blue jerseys with yellow letters!" Susan flashed a grin at Joannie. "At least for the ninth-grade cheerleaders."

"Hey!" called Michelle. "What about us?"

"Gray jerseys with navy blue letters," Susan said.

All the seventh- and eighth-graders groaned. I made a mental note to stop by Stone's myself and ask about changing our colors.

"Thanks, Susan," Beth Ann said. "Anything else about the powder-puff game?"

Cassie shot me a look. I knew she thought we should say something about what had happened with Kiri. But I shook my head. Why get everybody all upset about something nobody was going to notice anyway?

Patti raised her hand. "We've made the challenge posters," she said. Then she and Lauren held up a huge piece of bright yellow tag board. On it, in bold, royal blue letters, they'd written the challenge chant I'd given them:

HEY, NINTH GRADE!
GET READY FOR DEFEAT!
SEVENTH GRADE AND EIGHTH GRADE
NEVER WILL BE BEAT!
***

BE THERE TO SEE IT HAPPEN!

"No way!" All the ninth graders called out. "You wish!"

"Wait just a second," Patti said. "There's another one." Now she and Lauren held up a second yellow-and-blue poster:

SEVENTH GRADE, EIGHTH GRADE,
WE'LL PUT YOU TO THE TEST!
NINTH GRADE RULES!
YES! WE ARE THE BEST!
***

WITNESS THE SPECTACLE!

"Witness the spectacle?" Michelle giggled.

Lauren and Patti looked over at me, the author. I just shrugged. "Hey, why not?" I said. "It's going to be spectacular!"

"So," Patti went on, "if these are okay, we're ready to put them up. They fit on the bulletin boards in the front entrance."

"No need to vote on the posters!" said Susan. "Go hang them up. Then get back here pronto. We've got cheers to practice!"

*   *   *

47

BRRRRING!

My alarm went off at six-thirty on Wednesday morning.

I have to get up, I told myself as I fumbled to hit the clock and stop the awful ringing. I have to!

But I didn't.

I was exhausted from making phone calls about the powder-puff game. Organizing an event wasn't easy! And then I stayed up late to finish my math homework. My head hit my pillow again, and I fell right back to sleep.

And so Wednesday turned out to be just like the day before. Except I made extra sure to check that my clothes were on frontward. I looked great in my big black knobby-knit sweater, my tan leather miniskirt (a genuine sixties original!), my black-and-tan striped tights, and combat boots. Even if I felt only half-awake all day.

That night, before I went to bed, I took precautions. I put the alarm clock on my dresser all the way across the room. When it rang, I'd *have* to get out of bed! Then I called Lauren.

"Hi, Laur," I said. "I need a favor from an early riser."

When she was on the Paxton gymnastics team, Lauren had lots of early morning practices. She was still in the habit of getting up super early.

"What's going on?" she said. "You want a wake-up call?"

"Yep. If I don't make it to one of the Brick's fun-with-algebra-at-dawn sessions, she'll think I'm not trying."

"How's it going?" asked Lauren. "Any better?"

"You really helped me a lot," I said. "I can definitely do all the problems with inequalities that we worked on."

"That's good," she said. "You'll get the others, Tara."

"Yeah, well, I hope so. Anyway, call me at six-thirty."

"No problem," said Lauren.

"And when you call," I added, "don't just say 'Hi, bye.' Talk to me until you're sure I'm really, really awake. Okay?"

"Got it," said Lauren.

"Thanks, Laur," I said before we hung up. "I owe you one."

It worked! Between my alarm clock ringing and Lauren calling, I walked into the Brick's room on Thursday morning at seven-forty-five. Boy, did Ms. Brickman ever look surprised! She went over four types of problems that morning, and I really and truly understood them all.

The math session ended a few minutes before school began. I ran down to the ticket table to see how things were going. Michelle and Lauren told me they'd sold tons of tickets!

Thursday was turning out to be an okay day.

Until the end of lunch period. Then I got the jolt

49

that made me think it would have been better if I'd stayed in bed.

Patti and Lauren ran up to me as I walked out of the cafeteria.

"Tara!" cried Lauren, waving something in my face. "You won't believe what a horrible editorial Kiri wrote!" She thrust the paper at me. "Here. Read it!"

"This would *never* happen in Dallas," Patti was saying.

I grabbed the paper and started reading:

THE POWDER-PUFF PROBLEM

To raise money to attend a cheerleading clinic over spring break, the PJHS squad plans to sell tickets to a cheerleader vs. cheerleader "powder-puff" football game. Do the cheerleaders know how to play football? No! Are they trying to learn? Not at all. The whole thing, according to seventh-grade cheerleading alternate and organizer of the event, Tara Miller, is "done for laughs." Laughs? What's funny about students playing a game badly? Not much.

Isn't it interesting that the cheerleaders chose to call their event a "powder-puff" game? A powder puff is a soft, fluffy pad used for applying powder to the skin. The rarely used term brings to mind the days when women themselves were considered soft and fluffy.

Well, wake up, cheerleaders! You may consider yourselves a soft and fluffy part of the past, but most of today's female junior high and high school

50

students want to be taken seriously as women and
as future professionals.

In planning a "powder-puff" game, the cheerleaders have taken all women a giant step backward. There's only one way to show that the rest
of us know better. And that's by *not* buying a
ticket to the game—a ticket back to yesterday.

As my eyes skimmed Kiri's words, I felt my face
getting hot and then hotter. Why did she have to mention *my* name? And how could she tell people not to
buy tickets?

"It's nasty, all right," I said to Patti and Lauren. "But
nobody's going to pay any attention to it. Are they?"

"Who knows?" Lauren said. "We just set up the
ticket table again. Cassie and Michelle are there." She
grabbed me by the arm. "Come on. Let's go see if
they're selling any tickets."

We ran down the hallway. When we turned the corner, I couldn't believe my eyes. A *huge* crowd was gathered around the ticket table. It looked as if ticket sales
were booming. But as I hurried closer, I realized I was
wrong. Very wrong.

CHAPTER
9

We are *not* taking down these signs!" Cassie was saying to the crowd of maybe fifty kids who were gathered around the ticket table. "We have every right to sell tickets for our game!"

Up in front of the crowd was Darcy Lewis. She was the one who'd been so mean to Patti on the first day of cheerleading clinic. As usual, Darcy was surrounded by a little posse of girls who wanted to be just like her. They even dressed the way she did—in whatever outfit was in the window of the Gap that week. Not too original!

Naturally Darcy would be against our game. She'd be against anything the cheerleaders were doing. She'd been desperate to make the squad. But on tryout day, she refused to have spotters, so she'd been disqualified.

But then I saw that Darcy wasn't the only one arguing with Cassie.

"Don't you understand Kiri's editorial?" asked a tall girl in a green sweatshirt. "Don't you get it?"

"I don't think they do," said a redheaded girl. "Or they wouldn't be selfish enough to go ahead with this game."

"Don't you see how you've insulted women?" asked Annie Goff.

Annie was the smartest one in my math class. I didn't like to think that she was against us, too.

"No, I don't," said Cassie huffily. "All I see is that we're trying to raise money to go to a cheerleading clinic."

Now I jumped into the fight. "This game is supposed to be just for fun. Kiri didn't get *that!*"

"We're not thinking about fun," said the girl in the green sweatshirt. "We want to be taken seriously!"

"You don't even know how to play football!" said the girl with the glasses.

"Yes, we do!" Patti called out. Boy, she was angry! I'd never seen her face such a bright pink. "You better not say that till you see us play!"

"We're not coming to see you play!" called another girl.

"So don't!" I called back. "Don't buy a ticket! But move away from the ticket table. Make room for people who *do* want to buy tickets!"

"Right!" Michelle said vigorously. "Tickets are *on* sale!"

With plenty of grumbling, several of the girls walked off.

"Step right up!" called Michelle. "Get your red-hot tickets here! Get your tickets while they last!"

Then lots of kids did step up—girls as well as boys.

53

And they bought plenty of tickets. Patti, Lauren, and I pitched in, helping Michelle and Cassie sell tickets and make change.

Just as I'd handed someone a five-dollar bill, Emily Greer said, "Tara?"

Emily had come to the cheerleading clinic in August, but she hadn't made the squad. She'd been Darcy Lewis's partner and had been disqualified when Darcy wouldn't use spotters. But Emily got smart. She stopped hanging around Darcy and the other let's-all-dress-alike popularity seekers. She went out for the field hockey team—and made it.

"I just wanted to say good luck," Emily said.

"You mean with the football game?" I asked her, and when she nodded, I said, "Yeah, thanks."

"I think the game's a cool way to raise money," Emily went on. "If you need some help—like passing out programs at the game or something—tell me. I know all the girls on the hockey team are behind you guys."

I smiled. "Thanks, Emily. Thanks a lot. And if I can think of anything—you're on!"

As Emily walked away, I noticed that the crowd was thinning out. "How many tickets do you think we sold, Michelle?" I asked.

"I'd have to check the numbers on the tickets to be sure," she said. "But lots. And lots of the kids who bought them said they were doing it because they thought Kiri's editorial stank. She gave us the best publicity in the world!"

"All right!" I shouted. "Thank you, Kiri!"

I helped Michelle gather up the unsold tickets then. We put them into the cashbox along with a stack of five-dollar bills.

As I turned to go to class, Susan Delgado, Joannie Nichols, and Heather Smyth walked up to me.

"We hope you're not upset by what Kiri wrote in the paper, Tara," Susan said.

"I was upset," I said. "But not anymore. It sold tickets!"

Susan smiled. "That's great!" she said. "Listen, I've known Kiri since first grade. She always goes sort of overboard when she believes she's got a righteous cause."

"Don't worry," said Heather. "It'll all blow over."

"Right," added Joannie. "By the day of the game nobody will remember her little article was ever written!"

I grinned at the ninth-grade cheerleaders. "Thanks for saying that, guys," I said. "Thanks a lot!"

As I ran to my locker to get my Spanish book, I felt pretty good. Then I found a missing homework assignment folded inside the back cover. It was looking like my lucky day.

But as I hurried into class—slightly late, as usual—kids who'd been talking suddenly stopped. Everyone stared at me.

We speak only Spanish in class. No English is allowed. So I said, *"Hey! Qué pasa?"* which means "What's going on?"

"Hola, Señorita Miller," our teacher said as I sat down at my desk. *"Más vale tarde que nunca."*

The translation is "Better late than never!" Mr. Bochin said it to me almost every day!

"*Sí, Señor Rochin,*" I answered.

Then somebody sitting in the back of the room called out, "*Hola, Señorita Powder Puff!*"

I whipped my head around to see who'd said that. "*Señorita qué?*" I said to whoever it was.

Lots of kids were laughing.

"*Señorita Powder Puff!*" someone else called.

I felt my face growing warm. "*Cierra la boca!*" I said. That means "Shut your mouth!"

"*Basta,*" said Señor Bochin. *Enough.*

I checked the book of the kid sitting next to me to see what page we were on. I turned to that page, thinking how, for once, I agreed with Señor Bochin. *Basta!*

But it wasn't *bastante.* Not for lots of kids at PJHS. When Spanish class ended and I walked down the hallway on my way to math, I got lots of dirty looks.

"Cancel the game!" a girl called out to me.

"Say no to powder puffs!" called a boy walking with her.

Another girl called, "We don't want a ticket to yesterday!"

"What's the matter? Can't you think up your own line?" I called across the hall to her. "You have to quote Kiri Kelly?"

But worst of all were the kids who didn't say anything. They just patted their faces, pretending to powder their cheeks. I gave them nasty looks—as nasty as I could. I was almost glad when I made it to math class!

But not for long.

56

"Please place all books, notebooks, and papers inside your desk," Ms. Brickman said.

"Oh, no!" we all groaned. "We're having a test?"

"A quiz," the Brick corrected. "Please clear your desks."

Please let it be on inequalities, I pleaded. The Brick walked up and down the aisles. She put a quiz on each desk. When mine arrived, I scanned the problems. There were plenty of xs and ys and even some zs. There were parentheses and every operation sign ever invented. But no inequality signs anywhere.

"You have fifteen minutes," the Brick announced. "Begin."

Taking a deep breath, I started in on that first problem. I did the best I could. Before I knew it, Annie Goff was walking up and down the aisles, collecting the quizzes. As I handed her mine, I had a bad feeling that my best hadn't been good enough.

T.D. caught up with me outside the Brick's room after class.

"Nasty quiz, huh?" he said.

"The worst."

"Hey, I saw that stupid thing in the paper," he said. He started walking with me toward my locker.

"Yeah," I told him glumly. "I had no idea anybody read those editorial things. But I guess they do."

"But," T.D. said, "you're still having the game, right?"

"Right!" I told him. I reached my locker. T.D. stopped beside me. I started twirling my combination lock. "You think we'd let this stop us? No way!"

"That's good," he said. "You know, I think some of the girls will make pretty decent football players."

"Really! Kiri doesn't know what she's talking about. Patti and Lauren *are* good." As I opened my locker, an idea hit me. "Hey! Maybe we could *all* get good. If . . ."

"If what?"

"If you guys on the football team practiced with us! Would you? How about after your regular practice today?"

T.D. grinned. "Sure. I'll stick around. I'm sure Drew and Justin would toss the ball for a while."

I grinned back. "Great!"

T.D. began walking with me toward the gym. "Let's see," I said. "Today's Thursday. I'm sure Beth Ann will let us end practice early. We'll come out at the field at about four-thirty. Okay?"

"Okay," he said. "I'll tell Coach. Maybe he'll stick around, too, and give you a few pointers."

"This is going to be really good," I told T.D. with a wave. "Thanks, T.D. Thanks a bunch."

He started to turn down the hallway to the boys' locker room. Then he stopped. "One thing," he said.

"What's that?"

"You toss the ball with me," he said. "I'll show you how to do it right."

"Yeah, okay," I said, smiling. "See you!"

I headed for the girls' locker room to change for practice, thinking about T.D. The more I thought about what he'd said, the more I smiled. T.D. would *never* have said that unless he liked me, right? It seemed as if my on-and-off T.D. crush was about to switch to *on.*

CHAPTER 10

I checked my long-sleeved raspberry leotard, turquoise bike pants, canary-yellow socks, and white cheering sneakers in the locker room mirror. Slipping a rainbow of different-colored scrunchies on my ponytail, I was ready. Cheerleading practice, here I come!

But as I jogged for the door, a dark thought popped into my mind. What if I'd failed that math quiz? What if the Brick turned my grades in to the principal's office? If I had—and if she did—this could be my *last* cheerleading practice ever!

Well, I hadn't watched *Gone With the Wind* a hundred times for nothing. Like Scarlett O'Hara, I'd just think about *that* tomorrow!

Running over to our usual spot under the basketball hoop, I sat on a mat with—guess who? Lauren, Patti, and Cassie. I couldn't wait to tell everybody about going out to the field to practice football with the team!

"Okay, cheerleaders," Beth Ann said to start our meeting. "We've got lots to talk about before practice today. I guess we should start with the powder-puff game. And the editorial in the school paper. Susan?"

Susan stood up. "Personally, I think Kiri went a little overboard in her column. . . ."

"That makes two of us!" Deesha called out.

"Three!" I chimed in.

"Four!" said Lauren.

"I'm in for five!" called Patti.

I looked at Cassie, thinking she'd say *six*. But she didn't.

"And," Susan went on, "everywhere I went today, I got kidded about the name of our game." She gave her cheek a little pat.

Lots of girls called out, "Yeah! Me, too!"

"So we'll take some kidding." Susan shrugged. "Big deal. We'll do it with good spirit and show we have a sense of humor." She sort of waggled her eyebrows as she added, "Unlike some people I could name."

We all laughed at that!

Then Andrea White spoke up. "Susan?" she said. "What Kiri wrote *was* extreme. But it made me wonder about this game."

"Kiri had a point," said Jane Underhill, another ninth grader. "Powder puff isn't the image we want for our squad."

"Really!" called out Isabel Greenburg. "All of our tumbling passes and difficult stunts and dance numbers have nothing to do with being soft and fluffy!"

Several girls cheered Isabel's speech.

Susan was nodding and listening. "Well, is it the

name *powder puff* that's the problem?" she asked. "Or the game?"

"It's the name," all the ninth graders agreed.

"Okay, powder puff is out," Susan declared. "How about the ninth graders think up a name for our team and the seventh and eighth graders think up a name for their team? That way we can call the game by the team names. So ... start thinking, guys! Ninth graders, call me with suggestions. Everyone else, call Tara."

"We may have to take some teasing because of what Kiri wrote," said Joannie as she glanced my way. "But as Tara pointed out to me, Kiri also gave us some great publicity."

"Good point!" Susan exclaimed. "We have to remember that the most important thing is selling tickets. We've *got* to make enough money so we can go to that clinic!"

"Right!" almost everybody called out then. Susan sat down.

Well, *that* was over. Now it was time for my announcement.

When Beth Ann called on me, I said, "Besides going ballistic over the name powder puff, what Kiri sank her teeth into"—*like a pit bull,* I thought, but didn't say—"was the idea that we're awful at playing football. That we'd make fools of ourselves."

"Really!" Michelle called out. "How does she know?"

"We can change the name of the game—no big deal," I went on. "But nobody's ever seen us play. So how does Kiri know we're so bad at football?"

"Maybe we aren't!" Deesha said.

"Right!" I grinned. "And if we practiced with the football team—if they showed us some plays—we could look pretty good out on the field." Then I told them all about going out to toss the ball with the team after practice.

"That's great, Tara," Beth Ann said. Then she clapped her hands. "Now, let's start our practice. We've got a game to cheer for tomorrow!"

We all jumped up then and got into our practice groups. We put all our energy into forty-five minutes of cheering. At four-thirty we grabbed our backpacks and ran out to the field.

"Cheerleaders, line up and spread out!" said Coach Marzollo, who had stuck around to work with us.

Deesha told me that Coach Marzollo had coached the PJHS football team when her *mother* was a student here! Now he seemed sure he could coach our squad into a working football team.

I got into line between Patti and Cassie. The boys lined up about ten feet across from us. They each had a football. T.D. walked over and stood into line directly across from me. Drew positioned himself across from Patti. Big Justin Dubow stood next to Drew, across from Cassie, Lauren was down the line across from Michael Davis, captain of the PJHS football team.

"We're going to start today with a little passing and catching practice," Coach Marzollo said. "The correct way to hold the ball is with your fingers on the laces, like this."

He held up a football to demonstrate.

"The correct way to catch a ball is with two hands," he went on. "Like this."

Coach tossed the ball to Michael Davis. He caught it with both hands, spun it around until his fingers were on the laces, then fired it back to Coach.

"Okay," Coach said. "Let's see you toss and catch. Remember, keep your eyes on the ball."

"Ready?" T.D. called to me. Then he drew his arm back and threw the ball. I watched it spiral up and over to me. I put up my hands and caught it.

"Nice catch!" T.D. cheered.

We tossed the ball easily back and forth then. Even though I don't think of myself as a jock, I did okay. The whole time I kept my eyes on the ball—and only once in a while on T.D.

But I kept my mind on Kiri. Boy, was she going to be sorry she'd given us so much trouble about this game. Once we'd figured out what to call it, it was going to be a BIG event!

Then, just as I was checking to see that my fingers were on the laces, Cassie came flying in my direction. She practically knocked me down!

"Justin!" she exclaimed, getting to her feet. "Don't throw it *at* me, okay?"

"So how do I throw it *to* you without throwing it *at* you?" he asked.

"I don't know," Cassie said huffily. "Just do it."

On the other side of me, Patti was tossing the ball back and forth with Drew. She looked like a total pro.

"Hey, you are good!" I called to her. "Maybe you should go out for the team!"

"Watch Lauren," Patti said, and I looked down the line.

"Wow," I exclaimed as I watched her throw a long pass to Michael Davis. "She's *great!*"

"T.D.!" I called, jogging over to him. "Break time, okay?"

"What?" he said. "You think you've got it down already?"

"No," I told him. "I just want to check out my team before it gets too dark. I want to see who's really good."

Together, T.D. and I watched the passing and catching. Coach told the boys to back up a step each time they passed the ball. Pretty soon the cheerleaders really had to put some muscle behind their passes.

"Patti's really good," T.D. said to me in a low voice. "Deesha looks good, too. So does Michelle. Lauren could start for the Lions. Look at the way she gets her arm back!"

I nodded.

"But that girl"—he pointed at Christina O'Connor, who was ducking down or protecting her face with her arms each time Brian Lun threw the ball to her—"and Cassie—they should only go in if you're leading by about sixty points."

After Coach demonstrated kicking and running, we checked out the ninth graders. Susan, Heather, Joannie, and Isabel were handling the ball as if they'd been doing it all their lives. Andrea and Jane weren't bad, either. It was going to be a close game!

T.D. and I stood there for a few minutes watching

the cheerleaders practice football. What I saw was unbelievable! Everyone was taking this seriously. On a chilly afternoon after a whole day at school and a hard cheerleading practice, the Paxton cheerleaders were putting all their energy into learning to pass and kick and run with a football—all to make money so to get to a cheerleading clinic. As I watched, it seemed to me that we were exactly the opposite of how Kiri had described us in the paper.

CHAPTER
11

My left ear is killing me!" I complained to Mom when she walked in the door from work that night.

"Oh, sweetie! I can see how red it is. I wonder if we've got any ear drops."

"Drops won't help," I told her. "It's sore because it's been pressed against the phone for the last four hours!"

"Tara!" Mom laughed.

We sat down at the counter and ate some leftover Italian take-out from the night before. I told Mom all about practicing football.

"We are looking semiprofessional," I told her. "Some of us are anyway. But the name *powder puff* is out. That's why I've been on the phone all night. Everybody's been calling me to suggest a team name. But . . ." I shook my head. "So far they're all awful."

"Let's hear what you've got," said Mom.

I hopped off my stool and grabbed the sheet of note-book paper where I'd written down all the suggested names:

Seventh and Eighth Grade Champs	The Gridiron Girls
Seventh and Eighth Grade Killers	The Fighting Fems
Lucky Sevens and Eights	The Paxton Lionesses
The Paxton Panthers	The 7/8 Champs

"The Paxton Lionesses get my vote," Mom said. "I remember reading somewhere that in a pride of lions, it's actually the lionesses who do the hunting. The lions sleep all day."

"No kidding," I said, circling *Paxton Lionesses* on the list. "So could you say that calling the team the lionesses is a positive feminist statement?"

"It's a bit of a stretch." Mom smiled. "Sounds as if you've been working full speed ahead organizing this game, sweetie. Can I hope that you've also found time for some homework tonight?"

"I did most of it," I said. "Just not the math. . . ." I hadn't told Mom about how truly horrible my math grade was. But had to. What if Mrs. Weinstock sent Mom a notice that I had a sub-C math grade? But before I could start, the phone rang. Saved by the bell!

"Hi, Laur," I said when I heard her voice. "What do you think of calling our team the Paxton Lionesses?"

"I love it!" Lauren exclaimed.

"Yeah! Me, too."

"Listen, Tara," Lauren said after we'd talked a while, "I think the four of us should go talk to Kiri tomorrow."

"You're kidding."

"No," Lauren said. "Let's tell her we think she was right about the name 'powder puff.' And how we're renaming the game and how we're practicing really hard."

"What good will that do?" I asked.

"Maybe if she knows we're serious about playing a good game," Lauren explained, "she'll write something positive about us in next week's paper."

"I guess that makes sense," I said slowly.

"If she did that," Lauren went on, "maybe everybody would forget all about the other things she wrote."

"Okay, I'll go talk to her," I told Lauren. "But I have a funny feeling it's not going to be that easy."

"Come on, Tara!" Cassie exclaimed, running up to me as I walked into school on Friday morning. "Hurry up!" she urged. "Or we won't have time to talk to Kiri."

I'd arrived at school super early—for me. But naturally Cassie'd beat me. We were dressed in our cheerleading uniforms—blue and white sweaters with a big yellow *P* on the front, and blue pleated skirts with yellow and white triangles inside the pleats. That afternoon the Lions had a game against the Riverview Rams.

As Cassie and I raced down the hall, I thought about math class. If Ms. Brickman turned in my grades, I might *never* wear my uniform again! Then on game days I'd have to dress in my regular school clothes. (Not that everybody would call what I wore regular school clothes!)

Lauren and Patti were waiting outside the *Pax News*

office. The four of us marched into the room, past Brad Benton, who, today, was wearing a green plaid flannel shirt. We hurried straight to Kiri's door and knocked.

"Come in!" Kiri called. As we walked through the door, she added, "I thought I might see some cheerleaders in here today."

She was wearing a white turtleneck covered with teensy-weensy blue flowers. It looked like one I'd had in second grade! She also had on a blue cloth-covered headband. Luckily, she was sitting behind her desk, so I was spared from seeing what she was wearing on her lower half.

"We just wanted to say that you were right about the powder-puff image," Lauren told her.

Kiri looked sort of startled.

"Powder puff is out," Lauren added. "We're changing the name of the game."

Kiri began seesawing her pencil up and down between her thumb and first finger. "Just the name?" she asked. "You mean you're still having a football game?"

"Sure," Patti piped up. "Coach Marzollo is working with us. Wait till you see the plays we can do out there on that field!"

Kiri stopped jiggling her pencil. "What are you calling the game now?" she asked.

"We're still working on the name," Lauren said.

"We're open to suggestions," I added.

"We thought you might want to do a story on the game now," Cassie put in. "To let people know it's different."

"You just don't get it, do you?" Kiri said calmly.

"Get what?" Patti asked.

"Do you really think anybody would buy a ticket to your so-called game because they want to see the sport of football?" Kiri asked. Then she answered her own question: "I don't think so."

"But it's not *just* the name that's different now," I protested. "Because of what you wrote, we're not playing for laughs any more. We've challenged the ninth grade cheerleaders to a serious football game. What have you got against that?"

"There's no way you can play serious football!" Kiri said.

"Yes, we can!" Patti exclaimed. "We're practicing every day. We're learning all sorts of plays. This is serious!"

"No, it isn't," Kiri insisted. "Maybe you'll practice a few times. But that won't make it a serious game. It's like . . ." She pressed her lips together, thinking. "I know," she said at last. "What if the *Pax News* staff decided to raise money by holding a cheerleading demonstration? Would you take us seriously?"

That stopped us for a minute.

"Well," I said at last, "if raising money was what you wanted to do, would it really matter if I took it seriously? As long as I bought a ticket?"

"Of course it would matter!" Kiri shook her head. "What you do reflects on all the groups you belong to."

We must have looked as puzzled as we felt.

"As cheerleaders," Kiri began to explain, "what you do reflects on all other cheerleaders, on all other young women, on all PJHS students. You represent us. You represent *me*. Maybe you're willing to make fools of yourselves

70

playing football. But I don't want to be represented by fools. If women are going to be taken seriously, we have to act serious. And I'm not the only one who thinks so."

Kiri hunted through some papers on her desk. "Look at this petition," she said when she'd found a long sheet of paper. "A student came in here with it yesterday after school and asked us to run it as a full page in next week's paper."

At the top of the paper it said:

BOYCOTT THE CHEERLEADER GAME!
To the PJHS Cheerleading Squad:
The undersigned students will not attend a football game that makes fun of women!

Below it were at least fifty signatures of PJHS students. The first name on the list was Darcy Lewis. Of course she'd sign! But I read on. Annie Goff had signed. I hated to think that anyone as smart as Annie was on this list. I kept reading, name after name. It wasn't only girls who'd signed. Boys had signed, too. A lot of kids sure wanted to stop us from playing football.

"Did Darcy give this to you?" I demanded to know.

Kiri just shrugged. "I never reveal my sources," she said.

"I can't believe this!" Lauren exclaimed. "Are you really running it in the paper?"

"We have an editorial meeting this afternoon," Kiri said. "Unless you call off your game, I'm going to do my best to convince everybody at the meeting that we should run this petition."

71

CHAPTER 12

"*B*ut Tara!" exclaimed Cassie as the four of us stood together outside the *Pax News* office. "You'll be late for class!"

"I don't care," I said recklessly. "I've got to tell Beth Ann about this right now!"

"And Susan," Patti added. "We have to tell her!"

"You're right!" I exclaimed. "Susan's going to flip when she hears what Kiri's up to."

"Does anybody know what Susan's first-period class is?" asked Patti.

"She's got gym," Cassie said.

"I have science lab," Patti said. "It's not too far from the gym. I'll find her." And off she sped.

"I'm going up to Beth Ann's classroom," I said as the three-minute bell sounded.

"Now?" Cassie looked sort of shocked. "But—"

"We've got to stop *Pax News* from running that petition!" I turned and started up the stairs, taking them two at a time.

"I'm coming with you, Tara," Lauren said.

"Oh, me, too!" Cassie charged up the steps after us. "Even though I've never been late to class in my entire life."

Beth Ann's ninth-grade history class was all the way up on the third floor. By the time we got there, we were out of breath. We kept running, though, down to the end of the hall. As the eight-twenty bell rang, we skidded into her classroom, panting.

Beth Ann, cleverly disguised as Ms. Sorel, was wearing a silky green blouse and a deeper green straight skirt that stopped just above her knees. She had on silver earrings and a single strand of pearls. And no baseball cap! Standing up in front of her class dressed like that and wearing heels, our little cheerleading coach actually looked tall—and teacherly.

"What is it, girls?" Beth Ann asked, looking worried.

That's when I noticed that the whole classroom full of ninth graders was staring at us lowly seventh graders. Right in the front row sat Zack Kimmel. He was my friend Zoe's big brother. I'd had a crush on him since I was about six years old. I felt so stupid bursting into his history class like this!

"Um, Mrs. Sorel?" I managed. "Could we talk to you for a minute? It's important."

"Step out into the hallway," she told us. "I'll be right there." As we walked out the door, she added to her class, "Please review last night's reading on Thomas Jefferson and be prepared to discuss it when I get back."

73

"What's wrong?" Beth Ann asked as soon as she came out.

"Everything," I said, and we told her about the anti-football game petition. "We don't even know who started it," I finished up.

"But lots of kids have signed it," Lauren told her. "Kids I *thought* were my friends."

"Kiri says she's going to run the petition on a full page in next week's paper," I added. "Can she do that?"

Beth Ann looked thoughtful. "I suppose so," she said, "if the editorial staff and the faculty sponsor agree."

"But shouldn't whoever started the petition just give it to Susan or somebody on the squad?" I asked.

"That's right," Cassie said. "At the top it says 'To the PJHS Cheerleaders.' It's for us."

"Giving it to Kiri for the paper is different," I said. "It's so ... public."

"Really," Lauren agreed. "Putting it in the paper is *mean!*"

"Ohhh," I groaned. "How did a simple little money-making football game get to be such a big fat mess?"

Beth Ann smiled. "This game does seem to have created quite a stir," she admitted. "Well, look at the bright side."

"Which side would *that* be?" I asked.

"Big fat messes are part of life," she said. "Think of all the valuable experience you're going to gain handling this one!"

Beth Ann had us wait in the hallway while she went back to her desk and wrote hall passes for us.

"Don't worry, girls," she said as she gave them to us. "You'll figure out how to handle this. I have all the confidence in the world in my cheerleaders!"

"You know," Lauren said on the way back down the stairs, "what Beth Ann said made me feel better about everything."

"Definitely," I said, feeling slightly hopeful again. "We *will* figure out a way to handle this!"

"We *could* circulate an anti-anti-football game petition," suggested Lauren.

"Then someone would start an anti-anti-*anti*-football game petition," I pointed out. "But—hey! It's an idea!"

At the bottom of the stairs we stopped.

"You know, I'm still thinking about what Kiri said," Cassie told us. "How we represent all young women. It's sort of awesome, don't you think?"

"Not really," I muttered.

We split up then. As I walked to science class, my mind was spinning. I just had to think of a way to handle Kiri and this stupid petition. I just *had* to!

Word of the petition and Kiri's plans for it spread through PJHS that day faster than a chicken pox epidemic. I couldn't walk down the hall between classes without kids asking me about the game. Everybody asked the same question: Are you still playing that football game? And I gave them all the same answer: You bet!

In class I had trouble focusing on what my teachers

75

were saying. All I could think about was Kiri. Why was she trying to ruin everything?

By the end of the day I was in a daze. I didn't even see Beth Ann standing outside my math class talking to the Brick. I practically bumped into the two of them. Even then I just figured they were two teachers out in the hall, chatting about whatever teachers chat about.

Wrong!

"Tara," Ms. Brickman said as I started to walk into her classroom. "We'd like to talk to you for a minute."

Beth Ann put an arm around my shoulder. "Ms. Brickman has told me that you didn't do too well on your last math test."

My math grade! That quiz! Thanks to Kiri, I'd totally forgotten about what was, until this morning, my number one problem.

"But," Beth Ann went on, "she was kind enough to speak to me about it before she turned your grade in to the office."

"Thank you, Ms. Brickman," I managed.

"I think you know the grade policy for the cheerleaders," Beth Ann continued. "You failed yesterday's quiz, Tara. I'll have to suspend you from the squad until you bring your average back up to a C."

"I wish you'd come to more of the help sessions," the Brick said. "When you came yesterday, I felt you made real progress."

"I thought so, too," I told her.

"Tara has been working really hard for the cheerleaders lately," Beth Ann told the Brick. "She's been

76

in charge of our squad fund-raising project, which has run into a few snags."

"I love cheerleading!" I blurted out, and Beth Ann gave me a little squeeze.

"Well, I love math," the Brick said. "And I love it when my students pass the tests I give them."

"Do you have to suspend me?" I looked from Beth Ann to the Brick. "I'm alternate—I don't cheer at that many games. I could back off from the fund-raising project—I wouldn't mind that!"

Beth Ann laughed. But the Brick remained stone-faced.

"Policy's policy, Tara," Beth Ann said. "You need the time cheerleading takes to devote to math."

Then the Brick surprised me. "I might have a compromise," she said.

I was all ears!

"Your midterm exam is a week from next Wednesday," she went on. "I'll wait to turn in your grades until after that. But you'll have to go to the library for an hour every day after school and work with someone from our student math tutor program."

"Okay," I said quickly. Missing most of practice for over a week was bad. But it sure beat being suspended from the squad.

"I'll speak to a tutor this afternoon," the Brick said. "And don't think this is going to be easy. You'll have to score at least a B on the test to bring your grade average up to a C."

"I'll work hard, Ms. Brickman," I said. "Really I will."

"You'll have to," Ms. Brickman said crisply. "But I know you can do it, Tara. As I've told you before, you're a bright student. We'll begin on Monday."

"Beth Ann?" I said after Ms. Brickman went into her room. "Do the other cheerleaders have to know about this arrangement?"

She shook her head. "Just say you have my permission to miss practice. It's the truth. And it's all anybody needs to know."

After math class T.D. waited for me again. Justin and Drew waited with him.

"Walk fast," Drew said. "We've got a game, you know."

"We heard about the petition," T.D. said as we started toward the locker rooms.

"It stinks," muttered Justin.

"You think Kiri's really going to print it?" asked T.D.

"She says she is," I told them. "Unless we call off the game."

"If Kiri says she's going to do something," Drew said, "she does it. Her mom's the same way."

I squinted over at Drew. "You know Kiri's *mom?*"

"Yeah," said Drew. "She's my dad's sister. She owns this big company—Kelly Realty—and she is major-league bossy. Everybody's scared of her—even my dad."

I stopped so suddenly that T.D. practically tripped over me.

"What's wrong with you?" Drew asked. "Why are you looking at me like that?"

"Kiri's your cousin?" I exclaimed.

"Don't rub it in," he said.

"But you could talk to her!" I said. "Talk her out of putting the petition in the paper!"

"Oh, right," said Drew. "Mega-brain Kiri really pays a lot of attention to what I say."

"But you could try!" Even to myself I sounded desperate.

Drew just shook his head. "When Kiri thinks something isn't fair and starts going crazy over a cause," he said, "there's only one thing that'll stop her."

"What?" I practically shouted. "What is it?"

"Another cause," he said.

CHAPTER
13

"They're *cousins?*" Lauren said when I told her the news.

We were standing in the hallway, just across from the girls' locker room. We didn't have much time. The cheerleaders for the visiting team would be here soon. When they showed up, we'd let them have the locker room to themselves. So we had to hurry and grab whatever we needed out of our lockers.

"Can you believe it?" I said. Then I grew serious. "I have something else to tell you, Laur. Swear you won't tell?"

"Cross my heart," Lauren whispered back.

Quickly I told her about getting tutored in math.

"That's *great!*" exclaimed Lauren.

"I wouldn't go that far," I said.

"Well, I don't mean *great* great. But you'll get caught up in math. And you'll get to stay on the squad."

"I guess," I said. "I'll have to miss the first half of practice all this week. Part of next week, too."

"Don't worry," Lauren said. "If we learn any new stunts or cheers or anything, I can show them to you."

"Thanks," I said. "But if I'm two minutes late to practice, Cassie grills me like I'm some kind of cheerleading criminal."

Lauren giggled.

"So what's she going to do when I walk into the gym an *hour* late?" I wailed.

"Oh, Tara, you'll think up a way to deal with Cassie. Come on," she said. "We have to get ready for the game."

In the locker room Lauren and I squeezed down the aisle to our lockers at the end of the row. I sat down on the bench next to Patti. Lauren sat on her other side. Cassie was hunched over her locker, rummaging through her big bag of hair ribbons and scrunchies.

"We were talking about the petition, Tara," Aimee Adams said. "Some of us think we should cancel the football game."

"You're kidding," I said.

"I think we should cancel, too," Christina piped up.

"We can't let some petition stop us from going to the clinic!" Patti exclaimed.

"Besides," said Lauren, "we've sold tons of tickets!"

"We've already put so much effort into this game," I said. "I was on the phone last night for hours!"

"You're *always* on the phone for hours!" Michelle teased me.

"Not as many hours as last night!" I said, laughing. "I did permanent damage to my ear."

"There has to be a better way to raise money," said

Marie Bertolino, who was stepping into the Paxton Lion's mascot suit, "than playing all-girl football."

I folded my arms across my chest. "Name one thing."

But before anybody could, Susan Delgado poked her head into the aisle where our lockers were. "Listen up, guys!" she said. "We really need to talk about the game, all of us together."

"Right!" somebody called out.

"So I'm calling an all-squad emergency meeting for Monday morning, eight o'clock sharp in the gym. We'll figure out what to do about the game then. But right now we've got to get out there and cheer for the Lions!"

"That's right!" we all called out.

When the Paxton-Riverview game started, I sat on a bench down by the field. The other eighteen cheerleaders stood on the cinder track, leading a cheer. It was one that I'd made up.

> *Lions! Lions! That's our name!*
> *And tough is how we play the game!*
> *Now hear us roar!*
> *Now see us score!*
> *Lions! Lions! We want more!*

It was hard, sitting on the bench when all my friends were cheering. But I knew I wouldn't even be sitting on the bench if I didn't get my math grade up. I wished learning algebra were as easy as making up a cheer!

At the beginning of the second quarter, T.D. caught the ball and started running with it.

I jumped to my feet. "Go, T.D.!" I bellowed. "All the way!"

T.D. ran twenty yards before one of the Rams tackled him.

"All right, T.D.!" I yelled. "That's the way to do it!"

The Lions won the game, twenty to thirteen. As I walked back into the school to change, I thought how exciting it was to watch the games so close to the field. I couldn't bear it if I had to sit way up in the stands like a regular fan. I just had to get a B on that math test. I *had* to—no matter what it took!

Mom picked me up after the game, and we raced to the station. I just barely made the six o'clock train to Chicago. When I found a seat, I spent the whole trip leafing through three fashion magazines I'd picked up for the trip. Heaven!

The weekend flew by. On Friday night I sat for Lucy. To entertain her, I dressed her up in one of her mom's old tennis dresses. On her it's a floor-length gown. I accessorized with hair bows and tons of old costume jewelry. Lucy put on a fashion show for me, and I videotaped it. When Diane and Dad got home, they watched the tape and got a big kick out of it. Dad paid me ten dollars over my going rate. I guess that was his way of saying he appreciated my coming on Friday.

On Sunday Dad and I got dressed up. I wore a long forest-green V-neck sweater over a black short skirt, black lace stockings, and my high Doc Marten's. Just the two of us went downtown to brunch. I appreciated that. I love Diane, and Lucy, too. But sitting across the table from Dad and telling him all about cheerleading and the powder-puff mess was really great. It made me feel the way I used to in our old red convertible days.

On Monday morning—*early* Monday morning— Lauren stopped by to get me on her way to school. I was already up when she arrived. I was just having a little trouble getting it together.

"I can't wear this jumper without the belt," I griped, rummaging through a pile of clothes at the foot of my bed. "I mean, it's got these major belt loops."

Lauren dived into my closet. "Here," she said, dashing out with a narrow yellow belt. "Stick this through your loops and let's go! We can't be late for Susan's meeting."

Lauren was right—so even though the belt was totally wrong, I threaded it around my waist. Quickly I grabbed a granola bar and a juice box and we took off. We made it to the gym with a whole minute to spare.

"Let's start!" Susan called.

We all sat down on the mat. Beth Ann stood against the wall. Clearly she was letting us handle this problem.

"Okay," said Susan, "we're here to talk about our fund-raiser, the now famous all-cheerleader football game. As you know, it's taking some flak, and we're here to decide what to do about it. So—let's talk."

"Susan?" said Allegra Marshall, an eighth grader. "I don't think we should have the game. It's causing too much trouble."

"It could be great," added another eighth grader, Eva de Vos. "But I think Kiri's right about one thing.

84

We haven't practiced football enough to be very good at it."

"I agree," said Jane Underhill. "Maybe it isn't fair to ask kids to pay five bucks for a ticket to see something that's not really, really good."

Then Lauren said, "We can't give up raising money to get to the clinic! And this game could be totally awesome!"

"If we went out to the field and practiced every day until the game," Deesha Taylor said, "I think kids would *more* than get their five bucks' worth of football!"

"That's the truth!" Michelle called out.

"But what about that petition?" said Jane. "If Kiri puts it in the paper, it'll make us look bad."

"How?" asked Sara Feld. "We haven't done anything wrong."

"We're cheerleaders," said another ninth grader, Isabel Greenburg. "We're supposed to raise school spirit. This football game seems to be doing just the opposite."

Susan looked at her watch. Then she looked at me. "Tara? Any thoughts before we vote on what to do?"

This took me by surprise. So I blurted out what I felt: "I don't think we should let a newspaper piece or a petition or *anything* stop us from playing football!"

"All right!" lots of girls called out.

"Okay, let's vote," Susan said. "All in favor of having the game, raise your hand."

Patti, Lauren, Michelle, and Deesha put their hands up. So did Sara, Heather, and Joannie. With my hand, that made eight. Wait a minute! I whirled my head around to find Cassie. But when we made eye contact, she looked away.

I couldn't believe it! Suddenly that stupid scary old movie favorite of my mom's—*Invasion of the Body Snatchers*—flashed into my mind. Cassie'd been taken over by aliens! They'd made her a pod person! That's the only thing that could make her not vote for the game!

"Opposed?" said Susan.

Now the alien controlling Cassie's mind made her raise her hand. Kelsey voted no, too. So did all the eighth graders except for Sara Feld. Andrea, Jane, and Isabel made it a total of nine.

"I can't believe it!" Lauren wailed. "All those years of playing football with my brother could have paid off at last!"

Everybody laughed—even though Lauren was totally serious!

"Wait!" Patti cried. "Susan, you haven't voted yet."

"I only vote in case of a tie," Susan said. She sounded sad as she said it. "So I guess the no's have it. The all-cheerleader football game is officially canceled."

No one said a word after that. And no one moved to get up from the mat. I think even the girls who'd voted *no* must have felt sort of sorry.

"The game's over, guys," Susan said. "We'll make an announcement and start refunding ticket money tomorrow morning. But that doesn't mean we're not going to that clinic!"

Now we all jumped to our feet, cheering. Spontaneously we came together in a circle with our arms around one another's shoulders. All the bad feelings of who voted *yes* and who voted *no*—even my shock at Cassie's vote—seemed to disappear into thin air as we cheered.

Even though the three-minute warning bell is loud enough to wake the dead, we never heard it ring. Maybe we weren't going to play football, but we were still a together squad. After all, we were the Paxton cheerleaders!

CHAPTER
14

*T*ara!" Cassie called as I walked out of math class. I was only going to stash my books. Then I was going straight back to the math room. This was the first day of my tutoring. Cassie never met me after math class. Why was she here *today?*

"What?" I said. I sounded sort of cranky even to myself.

"We haven't had a chance to talk since the meeting this morning," she said. "I wanted to explain why I voted no."

"It doesn't matter," I told her.

"I want to tell you anyway," she said, following me down the hall to my locker. "Part of it was Kiri. What she said about us representing all young women really got to me."

"And the other part?" I asked.

Cassie looked sort of sheepish. "I *hate* playing football," she said at last. "I really, really hate it."

I had to laugh. "Well, that's honest," I said as we reached my locker.

"Anyway," Cassie said, "I've thought of another fund-raising idea, and I wanted to run it by you on the way to practice. If you think it's good, I'll tell Susan."

"Okay," I said. My mind was spinning. How was I going to explain that I wasn't going to practice?

"A concert!" Cassie exclaimed, beaming.

"Hey, not bad," I said, slamming my locker. "I've heard you can buy a block of tickets to the rock concerts at Andersen Hall for really cheap, and then resell them."

Cassie looked puzzled. "Actually, what I was thinking was we'd ask the school orchestra to play a benefit concert for us."

"Oh, that'd be a sellout," I said, rolling my eyes.

"It would be good experience for the orchestra," she went on, missing my sarcasm. "I could ask my father to announce. We might have to split the profits with the orchestra. But maybe we'd make enough to make it worthwhile. Well, should I tell Susan? What do you think?"

"I think," I said, "that you should keep on thinking."

"Oh." Cassie shrugged. "Well, it just sort of popped into my head. Anyway, let's get going."

"Um . . . you go ahead, Cass," I said. "I'm missing the first part of practice this week."

Cassie's eyes widened. "Missing practice?"

"It's cool," I went on quickly. "I mean, Beth Ann knows and everything."

"But *why?*" Cassie wanted to know.

"It's . . . uh, this math thing," I said. "Sort of an extra-credit type project for algebra."

"Oh, I know!" Cassie said suddenly. "For the state math competition, right?"

"Well," I said, "um, I think that's what it's called."

"Mr. Orlin wants me to take the test, too. I hear the trigonometry section is murder. No wonder Beth Ann is letting you miss practice," Cassie said. "It's a big deal to qualify. Congratulations!"

I started backing down the hallway.

Cassie waved. "Talk to you more about this later!"

Groaning, I headed back to Ms. Brickman's room.

"Well, this should keep you and your tutor busy for a couple of days," said the Brick. She stood at the door of her classroom holding a big fat folder filled with papers.

"A couple of days!" I exclaimed. "A couple of months is more like it! That folder looks like a telephone directory!"

I swear Ms. Brickman had to try *hard* not to smile.

As we walked silently together down the stairs, I wondered what was going on in the gym. I already missed being at practice.

Outside the library Ms. Brickman said, "I've asked one of my very brightest students to work with you, Tara. So I'm expecting great things of you on your test."

I opened the library door. My tutor was sitting alone at a round library table. Even though her back was toward me, I knew who she was. No one else at PJHS would wear a navy blue and green patterned sweater over a pair of red wool pants. No one!

Kiri looked around and saw me then. Her eyes

widened. I guessed she hadn't known who she was going to tutor, either!

"Whoa!" I said, stopping suddenly. "This is not going to work out, Ms. Brickman. No way."

"Yes way, Tara," Ms. Brickman answered me. "It is if you want to do well on my test and stay on the cheerleading squad."

Then my math teacher handed my math tutor the six-hundred-pound folder. The Brick turned and walked out of the library, leaving Kiri and me glaring at each other.

"Sit down," Kiri commanded briskly. "Let's start."

"Why are you doing this?" I asked, still standing.

"What, tutoring?"

I nodded. "Isn't running the school paper enough?"

"I like math, too," Kiri said, "so I joined the student tutors. Is that a problem?"

"No," I said. "Not if we just stick to talking about math."

That's what we did. We started with stuff I'd learned back in September. Back when I'd gotten an 82 on my test. Then we moved on to problems I was less sure of. Whenever I missed something, Kiri went through the problem step by step. As she did, I felt little lightbulbs clicking on inside my head.

I did so many sheets that afternoon, I thought my hand might fall off! But inside I felt pretty good. I was getting it!

I'd been checking my watch regularly. But Kiri actually caught me by surprise when she looked at her gold bracelet watch and said, "It's four-thirty."

I began shoving things into my backpack. I could still make it to an hour of cheerleading practice.

"Here," said Kiri, handing me even *more* sheets. "Do these tonight. Put them in my box at *Pax News* tomorrow morning."

"You're kidding," I said. "Right?"

Kiri gave me a blank look.

"Kidding," I said, imitating Kiri's voice. "It means joking, joshing, fooling around, just for fun. Ever hear of it?"

"You want to pass the math test or not?" was Kiri's answer.

"With all my heart." I stuffed the sheets into my backpack. "And you want to know why? So I can get my average up enough to stay on the cheerleading squad." I gave her an evil grin.

"My job is to help you understand the math," Kiri answered. "What you do if you get your grade up isn't any of my business."

"I wish you'd felt that way about our football game," I said. "You sure made *that* your business!"

"That was different. That involved the whole school. The paper is supposed to cover school issues."

I was itching to get to cheering practice. But I'd been thinking about what I wanted to say to Kiri for a long time. Now that I had a chance, I couldn't stop myself from saying it.

"I still don't understand why you were against us playing football. All we were trying to do was raise some money."

"Did you say *were?*" Kiri's eyebrows went up.

92

I nodded. "Thanks you and to whoever wrote that petition, we've canceled the game."

"I'm surprised," she said. "I didn't think you would."

"It was a close vote," I admitted. "But the unity of PJHS was more important to the cheerleaders than the football game."

Now Kiri frowned.

"What's wrong?" I asked. "I thought you'd be happy to hear that we're giving up our game."

"Oh, I am," said Kiri. "But without the petition I've got a whole page to fill in *Pax News.*"

"Well, how about a page wishing the PJHS cheerleaders good luck thinking up a new fund-raising idea?" I suggested.

Instead of answering me, Kiri frowned. "Why do the cheerleaders have to raise so much money, anyway?" she asked.

"I told you. So we can go to a clinic over spring break."

"But why is it up to your squad to earn the money for the clinic?" Kiri asked. "Why isn't there money in your budget?"

"We spent our money for the whole year going to the state competition last month," I said.

"Oh, I remember. We did a story about that," Kiri said. "Didn't you win something?"

"We came in third," I told her. "And third in the state isn't bad. Now, one more question, and then I'm going to cheering practice. What have you got against cheerleaders?"

"Cheerleading is antifeminist," she said.

"It isn't!" I protested. "Cheerleading takes total teamwork. We all support each other, big time! How can you say that?"

"Because it's girls standing on the sidelines while boys play a sport," she said. "Why shouldn't girls play a sport, too?"

"But lots of girls on the squad *do* play on sports teams." A sudden thought occurred to me. "What about you, Kiri? Have *you* ever played a sport?"

"Not really," Kiri admitted.

"Ask any of the kids on teams how they feel about having us lead cheers for them. They'll tell you how it pumps them up for the game."

Kiri nodded.

"And if their team is losing, having the cheerleaders on their side is a big boost for them to keep on trying!"

"I can see your point." Kiri sighed. "I guess the main thing that bothers me about cheerleading is that it's silly. All that jumping up and down and yelling. It's not dignified."

"You're right about that," I said, laughing. "It's definitely not dignified!"

Kiri smiled. "Well, you asked."

"But as for the 'jumping up and down' part," I said, "have you been to any football games this fall?"

"No, I'm not interested in football."

"How about a girls' field hockey game? We cheer there, too."

Kiri shook her head.

"So you haven't even *seen* us cheer?" I asked.

"Not really," Kiri admitted.

94

I stood up. "Kiri," I said, "now's your chance."

"I can't!" Kiri protested. "I have to go back to the *Pax News* office. I've got a million things to do."

"Make that a million and one," I told her. "This will take five minutes. After all you've written about the cheerleaders, the least you can do is come see us in action."

CHAPTER
15

"Okay, bases," Steve Liu was saying. "Elbows in tight. That's it, Deesha. Tighter, Kelsey."

No one noticed me peeking in the gym door.

"Come on," I whispered. I led Kiri over to the bleachers.

I could tell Kiri felt like she was coming into enemy territory. And in a way she was. Her editorial and her threat of running the petition had forced us to cancel our football game. At least eight of us on the squad were mad about that.

But I trusted the other cheerleaders to have a "wait and see" attitude. They knew me pretty well. Well enough to know that if I brought Kiri to practice, I must have a pretty good reason.

"Rest your arms against your rib cage, Deesha," Steve was saying. "Cassie? You feel secure up there?"

"Definitely," Cassie said.

"Don't arch your back, Kelsey," Steve said. "That'll throw the whole stunt off balance."

Kiri and I sat down. In a whisper I tried to explain

what was happening. "The girls on the floor are bases," I said. "Cassie's what's called a flyer. The stunt they're practicing is a double-based extension. That's two bases holding one flyer."

"It looks sort of dangerous," Kiri said.

"It can be," I told her. "But we learn the stunts step-by-step. And we have spotters," I added, pointing out how Eva was standing behind Cassie, with her arms up and ready—just in case.

"Over there," I said, "Beth Ann's working on arm movements. They have to be totally precise."

We watched a large group that included Lauren, Patti, and Michelle stand with their arms straight down by their sides. As they said the word *beware*, they jumped with their feet apart and brought their arms straight up over their heads.

"Hands in blades, Patti," said Beth Ann. "You're cupping."

They did it again. And again. Finally Beth Ann told them to go ahead and try the whole first line: *Beware Bobcats!*

"Take five," I heard Steve say. Within two seconds Cassie zoomed over to where we were sitting.

"Hi, Tara," she said. "Hi, Kiri. Um . . . what's going on? Have you been reviewing for the math com—"

"Right!" I interrupted her. Kiri looked confused. But before she could say a word, I quickly went on. "Cassie, you know Kiri's never seen us cheer?"

Luckily, Cassie took the bait. "Never? So, are you here to do an article on cheerleading for the paper?"

"It's possible," Kiri replied.

Cassie lit up. "Great! Hey, wait right here. We should give you something to write about."

I grinned as Cassie dashed off toward Beth Ann. "I think you're going to get a demonstration," I told Kiri.

"I hope it doesn't take too long," Kiri said. "I've really got to check on the paper."

"Don't worry," I said. "We cheer fast."

A minute later the whole squad began forming up on the mat.

"We're doing our competition cheers," Cassie ran over to tell Kiri. "The 'Hey, Indiana' cheer's first. It's incredible!"

"The jump at the end is called a flying split ripple," I explained. "You'll see why."

Susan called, "Ready, *and!*"

Indiana, our State!
We think you're great!

Next came the spelling part, where the girls alternated between jumping forward and back.

I - N - D - I - A - N - A !

"Here it comes!" I said to Kiri as the tallest cheerleader began the ripple of jumps:

Indiana! That's the way!

It ended with Lauren's incredibly perfect toe-touch. Kiri didn't exactly leap to her feet, clapping. But she turned to me, her eyes wide open, and said, "That was amazing. I had no idea that you did things that were so gymnastic."

"What?" I asked innocently. "You mean all this jumping up and down?"

"It's more than that," Kiri admitted. "A lot more."

After watching our other two competition cheers, Kiri clapped really hard. "I've got to go, Tara," she said then. "But thanks for bringing me in here. It was a real eye-opener."

After she left, everyone cooled down and we had a meeting.

"That was a surprise, Tara," Susan said.

"Maybe Kiri has a new appreciation of cheerleaders," I said.

"Really!" Susan said. "All right, Michelle? Anything to report on refunding the ticket money?"

"Lauren and I are setting up the ticket table inside the front entrance tomorrow morning," Michelle said. "Patti made us a sign in art class that says Refunds."

"Well, that should make it clear," Susan said. "Okay, that's it for today. Keep thinking of ways we can make some money, guys. The deposit deadline for the clinic is sneaking up on us."

As usual, I walked home with Lauren, Patti, and Cassie. Patti was meeting her mom at the radio station today. Lauren was coming over to study with me again.

"Bringing Kiri to practice was brilliant, Tara," Cassie said as we reached my apartment building. "And it is so cool that you guys are studying together for the math competition!"

"For the *what*?" Patti exclaimed.

"Didn't she tell you?" Cassie turned to Patti. "That's why Tara's missing practice. And after all that complaining about how much trouble she was having in math!"

"Tara, that's great!" Patti said.

I shot a glance at Lauren. She was biting her lip to keep from laughing.

"Bye, Patti! See you tomorrow, Cassie!" I said, making my escape into the courtyard.

"Bye, guys!" Lauren said.

Just inside the gate Lauren cracked up laughing.

"Stop it!" I said.

"I can't!" Lauren said, gasping for breath. "I mean, how could you tell her that, Tara?"

"I didn't tell her," I said, feeling sort of uncomfortable. "I just said I was working on a math project. She's the one who jumped to the conclusion that it was for the competition."

Lauren cracked up again. She didn't stop laughing until we got to my apartment.

It took me all of Monday night to finish my math sheets. On Tuesday morning I stuffed them into Kiri's box at *Pax News*.

When I walked into the library after school that day, I wasn't exactly looking forward to seeing Kiri. But I wasn't dreading it, either.

Kiri beat me to the library again. She had my already-graded math sheets in front of her. Ready for a fashion report? A red-and-white checkered blouse with a ruffle collar, and a matching red and white bow in her hair. Not good. It flashed into my mind that if she helped me get my math grade up, maybe I'd offer to take her shopping!

I sat down. It was hard not to bring up cheerleading practice. I wanted to hear Kiri say one more time how impressed she'd been. But I made myself wait until I'd gotten my daily dose of algebra. So I just said, "How'd I do on the sheets?"

"Here's where you're having problems," she said, and we started right in. We worked for one solid hour on math.

Finally Kiri said, "That's all I'd planned to cover today." She started digging around in her bag then. She was picking out more homework sheets for me. No! I couldn't take another night of nonstop math!

"Kiri," I said, "pack those sheets back into the folder now and nobody gets hurt."

"How else do you expect to catch up on a whole semester of math in a week and a half?" she asked, handing me a fat stack of worksheets.

I groaned and let my head drop to the table.

"They won't kill you," Kiri said.

"They might," I said, sitting up. "My mom doesn't get home from work until ten-thirty. Last night when she got home I *still* hadn't finished the math sheets."

Kiri tilted her head slightly. "My mom doesn't get home until late, either," she said.

"Yeah? I thought she was the boss of a whole company."

"She says bosses work harder than anybody."

101

"Well, my mom's not the boss," I said. "But she works six days a week and long hours."

"Mine, too," Kiri said. "If I didn't wait to eat dinner with her when she gets home from work, I'd never even see her."

"That's how it is for me, too," I said. "And we eat takeout every single night."

"Us, too," said Kiri. "I am so *sick* of lukewarm food."

We had a long conversation then about where our moms got takeout. We agreed that Uncle Thai's was the best Chinese, and I recommended the broccoli pizza from Gino's.

At last I asked, "Um ... does your dad live with you?"

Kiri shook her head.

"Yeah, mine either," I said. "He lives in Chicago with his other family. How about yours?"

"I've never met my father," Kiri said, her voice sounding suddenly small. "It's just me and my mom."

It was funny to think that Kiri and I had something in common. I mean, we didn't think alike—or dress alike!—but we both *loved* moo shu veggies!

As I stood up to go, Kiri got sort of a strange look on her face. "Can I come watch your practice again?" she asked.

"Sure!" I said.

"You don't have to sit with me or anything," she said as she grabbed a little notebook. Then the two of us walked down to the gym. While I changed into my cheering sneakers, Kiri started interviewing the other cheerleaders. She talked to Steve and Beth Ann, too. She watched everything. She even stuck around for our meeting—and took notes on that!

Maybe Kiri really is doing another article about the squad, I thought. But something about her question-asking and her note-taking and her eagle-eye watching made me nervous. Could we trust her to get it right this time?

CHAPTER
16

"**F**orget the sheets for a minute," Kiri said when I met her in the library after school on Wednesday.

I must have looked totally shocked.

"We'll get back to math," she assured me. "But first I have a couple of questions about the cheerleading clinic. Does going to such a clinic add to your competence as cheerleaders?"

"Sure. It's where all the squads in the state go to learn the latest stunts and spotting techniques and—"

"Spotting," Kiri said. "That has to do with safety, right?"

"Definitely."

Kiri broke into a smile. "I've discovered a gross injustice, and I've been doing some journalistic digging around."

"What does that mean?" I asked. "Spying?"

"Let's just say investigating. Can you keep a secret?"

"Cross my heart," I said out of habit. "I mean, sure."

"Great," said Kiri. "I think you and the other cheerleaders are going to be pretty interested in what I've found."

"So tell," I said. Drew sure had been right about his cousin. Kiri was on to a brand-new cause. It sounded as if the new cause had something to do with the Paxton cheerleaders.

Kiri pushed a sheet of paper across the table to me. On it were columns of numbers.

"What is this?" I asked. "The world's longest math problem?"

"It's budgets," Kiri said. "For all the school's extra-curricular activities."

"Speak English, Kiri."

"It shows that each year the football team gets more money than the cheerleaders."

"That doesn't surprise me."

"But they get *fifteen times* more!" Kiri said. "The cheerleader budget is tiny! It's down there with the chess club, which doesn't have uniforms or traveling expenses or anything!"

That's when it hit me that understanding math could actually be a useful thing in life!

"We have to show this to Beth Ann!" I said.

Kiri shook her head. "This is my scoop," she said. *"Pax News* will break the story of unequal funding at PJHS on Thursday."

"What got you started on this anyway?" I asked.

"What you said," Kiri answered. "About how you used up your whole year's budget going to the state competition. It just didn't seem right to me. If the school expects you to be first-class cheerleaders for the

PJHS teams, then they should put money in the budget to make it happen."

"You mean if we had a big enough budget we wouldn't have to worry about raising so much money."

"Exactly. It's too late to change this year's budget," Kiri said. "But there's always next year's."

I sighed. "Even if we get more money next year because of your story, we still have to raise the money to get to this year's clinic. We still need a great money-making idea."

Kiri looked thoughtful. "Well, after seeing the stunts your squad can do . . ." Her voice trailed off for a moment. Then she said, "When you cheer at football games, do you do the tumbling and gymnastics that you showed me?"

"We do some stunts," I said. "And at halftime we do a cheer with a pyramid. But what you saw yesterday was for a cheering competition. We can't do those cheers outside. We can only do them in a gym with mats and the right floors and things."

As I explained this to Kiri, I suddenly understood why she'd asked. "Only a few people at PJHS have ever seen us do the competition cheers," I went on, thinking out loud. "And we've been working on a couple of really great dance numbers, too."

Kiri and I stared at each other for a moment.

"We could put on a big cheerleading demonstration," I said.

"I'd definitely pay five dollars to see more of what I saw yesterday," Kiri said. "And the more people who see you—especially teachers and the principal—the

106

better chance there'll be for getting a bigger budget next year."

"You know, this could work," I said. "This could be huge."

Kiri checked the time. "We're twenty minutes late starting," she said.

"That's okay," I said. "I've just got to make it to the end of practice so I can bring up this idea!"

I amazed myself that afternoon. I actually focused on math for one whole hour. At the end of that time I could do five kinds of problems that had baffled me before.

"Thanks, Kiri!" I said just before I zoomed down the hallway. By the time I skidded into the gym, everybody was sitting down on the mats.

"That's all I have," Susan was saying.

"Hold it!" I said, running over. "Have you already talked about new moneymaking ideas?" I asked.

"We have," said Susan. "But we didn't really come up with anything workable. Why?"

Then I told them about the idea of putting on a big cheerleading demonstration.

"We've got the three cheers we did for the competition," I said. "And the dance numbers we're working on now."

"Hey! Michelle and I have been working on new dance," Deesha called out. "It's definitely something we could use."

"This could be a fund-raiser plus a celebration of the great football season we've had this year. And," I finished up, "nobody can say we haven't practiced cheering!"

"I know!" said Sara Feld. "Our last football game is a night game, on Saturday. What if we had the demonstration right before it? Then everybody'd be super pumped up for the game!"

Everyone cheered this idea.

"You know," Lauren said, "I can really picture us doing this!"

"Me, too," Cassie said. "Which is something I *never* could do with the football game."

"You know who's basically responsible for this idea?" I said. "Kiri! She said she'd pay five dollars to see more of what we showed her yesterday. Suddenly I thought, 'Hey, why not?'"

Everyone seemed to be nodding and getting psyched.

"But we've just finished refunding everybody's money from the powder-puff game," Michelle said. "Does this mean we have to start selling tickets all over again?"

The gym filled with murmurs as little group discussions broke out about the tickets.

"Why don't we just pass out flyers?" Patti suggested at last. "And sell tickets at the door?"

"That's risky," Susan said. "But I think it's the only way to handle it."

"Susan?" said Allegra. "The competition cheers are in great shape. And the two dances are coming along. But can we really pull together a whole demonstration in a week and a half?"

More murmurs started.

"We forgot about the cheer Tara made up for the kids at Memorial Hospital," said Kelsey. "We could do that!"

"Patti," Lauren said. "Maybe your mom could teach us that University of Texas cheer. The one that ends in the Herkie."

Patti rolled her eyes. "You know she'd *love* to!"

"Plus the dance Deesha and I made up," said Michelle.

"Beth Ann?" said Deesha. "Can we use our regular practices to get ready for this?"

"Fine," Beth Ann said. "I've just got one question. Why didn't you girls come up with this in the first place?"

We all laughed at that! Then Susan called for a vote. There were nineteen votes *for* the demonstration. Nineteen votes from nineteen cheerleaders who were determined to go to that clinic!

CHAPTER
17

"Kiri?" I said into the phone. I'd gotten her number from information. She had her own line. "Hi, this is Tara."

"Oh, hi." Kiri sounded a little surprised to hear my voice.

"I just wanted to tell you that the squad voted to do the demonstration," I said.

"Thanks for telling me. I'll mention it in my piece. It'll make a great ending."

"Great. And I told everybody how it was really you who came up with the whole idea."

"But you didn't tell them what I'd found out about the funding, did you?"

"Never!" I said in my all-purpose spy accent. "Do not worry, Kiri. Your secret is safe with me."

"It better be!" Kiri laughed.

"I also want to ask a favor," I said then. "If it's okay with Ms. Brickman, could you tutor me during lunch period?"

"I usually try to catch up on *Pax News* business at lunch time," she said. "What's wrong with after school?"

"The squad wants to work on the demonstration then."

Kiri was quiet for a minute. "Well, okay," she said. "I really want this demonstration to work out. It'll make my story much more effective. So come to the *Pax News* office tomorrow. But be prepared to work fast!"

"I will," I told her. "Thanks, Kiri. Thanks for everything!"

We hung up. Then I did something I've never done before in my life. I turned on our answering machine. I let it take every call that came in—all twenty-four of them! I was tempted to pick up—so tempted! Especially once, when I heard T.D.'s voice! But I gritted my teeth and didn't.

What I did was math sheets. I mean, what good would it do for me to get a really hot fund-raiser going and then get kicked off the squad?

Thursday was an amazing day! Thanks to a wake-up call from Lauren, I made it to the Brick's early morning torture session. At lunchtime I dashed to the *Pax News* office. Kiri and I whizzed through as many problems as we could. Brad Benton even brought us plate lunches from the cafeteria so we could keep going.

At the end of lunch period *Pax News* hit the halls. The cheerleaders were in the news again. We weren't in the editorial column this time. We were right on the front page.

THE PAXTON CHEERLEADERS:
BIG STUNTS ON A TINY BUDGET

That was the headline. The lead was how cheerleading had changed from the days when it was "jumping up and down and yelling" for boys' teams. Now, Kiri wrote, "it is a sport that demands drill-team precision, the agility of gymnastics, and incredible togetherness and teamwork."

Basically, it was a story about us. Kiri told how we'd taken third at the Indiana competition with twenty schools from all over the state. She'd even called the schools of the squads that had placed first and second. She'd found out that their budgets were the same or *bigger* than those of their football teams! It was amazing, she wrote, that PJHS had managed to place at all given our "tiny budget."

At the end of her piece Kiri mentioned my name again. But this time it was to give me credit for thinking up "the cheerleading extravaganza."

Extravaganza! Now *that* was a great word!

Kiri ended the article like this: "Go see the Paxton Cheerleaders in action. See if you don't agree that PJHS has an undervalued and underfunded resource in its cheerleading squad."

For the rest of the day it was hard to concentrate on anything! Kids in the hallways were calling out congratulations on the article and saying they hoped we'd get more money next year. Nobody was doing any cheek patting anymore. Nobody was calling anybody Señorita Powder Puff.

After school I ran toward the gym. Right outside the principal's office, I almost ran right into Mrs. Weinstock.

"Oops!" I exclaimed. "I'm sorry!"

"That's all right," Mrs. Weinstock said. "Oh, you're one of the cheerleaders, aren't you?"

"I'm the alternate," I told her. "I'm Tara Miller."

"Ah, the one in charge of the extravaganza," she said. "Well, I'll certainly be there to see it."

"That's great, Mrs. Weinstock," I said. "I hope you'll think we look like a million dollars!" What a hint, huh?

I raced on to the gym then. Cassie and I started sprucing up the first dance number. We were both in it. So were Deesha, Marie, Eva, Andrea, Joannie, and Isabel.

"Whooo-wheee!" shouted Patti when she watched us go through it at the end of practice. "You all could be Laker Girls!"

That night at dinner I practically fell asleep in my sesame noodles.

"Hey, Tara! You're not turning into a morning person on me, are you?" Mom joked just before I staggered into the pit and collapsed on my bed.

"Why, I'd be tickled pink if the Paxton cheerleaders practiced for the extravaganza in our cartwheel room!" Mrs. Richardson had said when Patti brought up the idea. She'd also agreed to teach us the U.T. cheer.

And so at noon on Saturday the whole squad showed up at Patti's house. Lauren and Cassie and I arrived a little early.

"Hi, Tara!" Patti's seven-year-old sister, Missy, greeted me at the door. Missy has a head of curly blond hair, and she always kind of bounces off the walls. Know what she did when she first met me back in August? She ran up to her room and changed her clothes so she'd look just like me! What a great kid!

"Come upstairs for a minute, Tara!" Missy said. "Mom and I made all my Barbies cheerleader outfits!"

That I *had* to see! When I came back down, I walked into the kitchen. Cassie, Lauren, and Patti were already there.

"I've made you girls a whole pile of sandwiches—ham, egg salad, salami, roast beef—and there are three pitchers of iced tea in the fridge," Mrs. Richardson was saying. "And if you want anything else, you just tell me."

"Sure, Mom," said Patti.

Mrs. Richardson looked at her watch. "I think I'll go upstairs and change before everyone gets here," she said.

"Mom?" Patti said. "Don't put on your old cheerleading uniform, okay?"

"Why, Patti!" Mrs. Richardson said. "That thought never even entered my mind!"

Missy agreed to answer the door. In fact, she was thrilled to do it. Everybody gasped as she led them back to the cartwheel room, with its wooden floors and big floor-to-ceiling mirrors.

By quarter after twelve the whole squad was in the cartwheel room. Several of the girls were actually doing cartwheels! Beth Ann and Steve showed up, too. Everybody was into the extravaganza being a hit!

"Let's start!" I yelled. As everybody quieted down, I thought how I was running the show again. Whether I liked it or not. "Today we want to go through the three competition cheers. Since Lauren didn't cheer at the competition, Steve's going to work with her so she'll know where she fits in."

"Lauren's agreed to try an Around the World!" said Steve.

Lauren looked kind of nervous. An Around the World starts out as a pike jump and goes into a toe-touch. It's hard!

"Then," I went on, "Mrs. Richardson is going to show us a cheer called 'We'll Show You How.' Let's hear it for Mrs. Sunny Richardson!"

We gave Patti's mom a hand. She stood in the corner of the cartwheel room, grinning from ear to ear.

"After that, if we have time," I continued, "we'll go through the cheer we did at Memorial Hospital, and we'll finish with the dance numbers. And . . . that's it."

"Tara?" Susan said. "Joannie and I came up with a dynamite way to start the demonstration."

"Great!" I said. "Let's hear it!"

She and Joannie explained what they had in mind. When they finished, we all jumped to our feet, clapping and cheering.

"Yeah!" said Susan. "We *thought* you might go for this little number!"

"But the only way it's going to work," added Joannie, "is if we can keep it to ourselves. Totally to ourselves."

"Right," said Susan. "This has got to be top secret."

Without thinking about it, I stuck out a hand, my palm facing down. Patti, Cassie, Lauren ran over to me. They each slapped on a hand. Then Susan added a hand, then Joannie, then Heather, then Jane, then everybody in that cartwheel room slapped on one hand and the the other.

"Here's to our little secret!" I said. Then I tried to pop that stack of hands into the air. It wasn't easy!

CHAPTER
18

"Not bad," I told my dance group after we'd run through our number maybe fifteen times. "But not good, either. Let's take it from the top. Places . . . and . . . hit it, Missy!"

Missy hit the Play button on the boom box. An instrumental rock song by the band Sisterhood blasted into the cartwheel room. I jumped up and ran into the line just as our dance began.

I knew we'd have to call it a day pretty soon. It was almost six. We'd been working nonstop since twelve-thirty. But before we quit, I needed to know that this number was working.

As the song ended, Missy ran off. In a minute she ran back into the cartwheel room.

"Is it just Paxton cheerleaders I'm supposed to bring back here, Tara?" she asked me.

"Why, Missy?" I asked. "Is somebody else at the door?"

"Uh-huh," Missy said. "But I'm not supposed to say who."

"It's us!" Drew Kelly announced as he, T.D., and Justin burst into the room.

"What are you guys doing here?" asked Patti, turning pink.

"We were shooting baskets in Drew's driveway," T.D. said as Justin homed in on the sandwich tray. "We saw everybody coming over here for a party or something. So we thought we'd crash."

"You're practicing for the extrava-gonzo, right?" said Drew.

"Do you have your cheers lined up and everything?" asked T.D.

"What these guys want to know," Justin told me, his mouth half full, "is whether they still get to be cheerleaders."

"But we're not playing a football game," I said. "We don't need cheerleaders. And we're not doing this thing for laughs."

But suddenly I remembered something Steve had said.

"Hey, Steve?" I called. And when he came over to us, I explained how we had two "volunteers" to be in the demonstration.

"Can you show them how to do some really cool stunts?" I asked him. "Stunts that we can't do with an all-girl squad?"

"You bet," Steve said. "I can pair you guys with some flyers. You won't believe what you can do! You'd have to work with us all next week, though. Are you into it?"

T.D. and Drew looked at each other. Then back at Steve.

"Sure," said T.D. "Only we've got a game right after the demonstration. So we can't break any bones or anything."

Steve turned to Justin. "For the stunts I've got in mind," he said, "it sure would be great to have three boys."

I thought Justin was going to choke on his third ham sandwich when he heard that!

"Not me," Justin said. "I'm not being a cheerleader."

"Aw, come on, Jus!" I begged him. "The other guys can't do it without you! Please, please, *please?*"

"Uh-uh," Justin said. "Not a chance. No way."

On Monday morning all nineteen of us on the squad arrived at school early. We began passing out the flyers that Patti and Cassie had made. Here's what they said:

The PJHS Cheerleaders
are proud to present
A CHEERLEADING EXTRAVAGANZA!
Nov. 28, 5:00 P.M. in the PJHS gym
Tickets $5, available at the door ... while they last!

Lauren's brother, Jed, and his girlfriend, Salleen Cook, passed out our flyers in the high school. Salleen is captain of the Paxton High cheerleaders. When she handed out the flyers, it really meant something!

At lunchtime I zoomed down to the *Pax News* office.

As I walked in, Kiri looked at her watch. "We have forty-five minutes," she said, "let's get started."

"Right," I said, handing her the math sheets I'd spent my entire Sunday finishing.

While I started in on a new sheet, Kiri checked my other sheets over.

"Tara, what's going on?" she said, frowning.

I looked up from my work. "Why? What's wrong?" I asked.

"These problems," Kiri said. "A lot of them are wrong!"

"You're joking!" I managed. "Well . . . help!"

"There's no one thing you're doing wrong," Kiri said, scowling over my sheets. "You've just made careless mistakes. Lots of them."

By the time lunch hour was over, I'd fixed those mistakes. But as Kiri handed me a new batch of sheets, I felt as if I'd just make new ones.

"Check the problems when you finish," Kiri said.

"Okay," I said. "But Kiri? The exam is day after tomorrow. You think I'll do okay?"

"You will," Kiri said. "Don't worry."

But as I left Kiri's office, I turned to tell her goodbye. I thought she looked pretty worried herself.

"Tara?" Ms. Brickman said that afternoon in math class.

I looked up. "Yes?"

"Have you found x yet?" she asked me, looking hopeful.

"I think so," I said. "Is it seven?"

Her smile faded. "Seven over two," she corrected me.

I looked down at my paper. Of course! "Okay, I get it," I said quickly. "It equals three and a half."

Ms. Brickman nodded. "Check your work, Tara," she advised. "That goes for the whole class."

I nodded. What had happened? What had gone wrong? I'd been making great progress with Kiri. But now I didn't seem to be able to do a single problem right! Had I become so involved with the extravaganza that I'd totally lost my focus in math? But I had to do both! I just *had* to!

"I thought I *auto* call you for a change," I told Dad when I phoned him that night.

"Hi, sweetheart," Dad said. "What's new with you?"

"The bad news is algebra," I said. "Just when I think I get it—I don't."

"It's hard, huh?"

"Really hard," I said. "My test is Wednesday. Keep your fingers crossed for me."

"They're crossed. What's the good news?"

"The cheerleading extravaganza is looking fantastic," I said. "Our principal, Mrs. Weinstock, is definitely coming. She's one of the people who decides the sports budgets. So if we want more money next year, we have to do a knockout performance!"

"It sounds great, honey."

"You and Diane and Lucy are still coming, right?"

"Well, Lucy had a sore throat all weekend," Dad

said. "We hope she'll be feeling up to a trip by Saturday."

"Dad! It's only Monday!" I protested. "Saturday's practically a whole week away. She'll be okay by then!"

"We're sure going to try to come and see you, sweetheart."

"Try hard, okay, Dad?" I said. "It's really, really, *really* important to me for you to be there."

A little fuchsia T-shirt. My black leather skirt with the silver studs down the seams. Fuchsia tights. Combat boots.

That's what I'd been wearing the day I got an 82 on my math test. (I always remembered what I was wearing!) That outfit had been lucky for me once. I hoped it would be lucky for me again. I pawed through my closet and my dresser drawers, searching for those tights. I'd studied for that math test all I could. My brain was swimming with formulas and weird little mystery letters. What I needed now was luck. Ah, here they were!

At two-ten that afternoon, I sat down at my desk in Ms. Brickman's classroom. I had two sharpened pencils and two hundred butterflies in my stomach. This was it. The hour that would determine whether I was a Paxton cheerleader. Or an ex-Paxton cheerleader.

"Place all book, notebooks, and papers inside your desk," the Brick said.

T.D. turned around in his seat. "Good luck!" he whispered.

"Yeah, thanks," I whispered back. "You, too!"

Then the Brick walked up and down the aisles, putting a test on each desk. When I got mine, I picked up a pencil, and for one solid hour I focused on math. Then I checked my work.

At three-ten, I placed my test in Ms. Brickman's in-basket. It was over! I didn't have it hanging over my head anymore!

I practically galloped out of the math room. And practically mowed down Cassie, Lauren, and Patti, who were standing outside, waiting for me.

"It's over! It's over! It's over!" I sang.

"What's over?" asked Patti.

I just kept singing, "It's over! It's over!" In my joy I picked up Cassie, book bag and all, and started twirling her around.

"Tara!" Cassie yelled. "Put me down! We have to talk to you about that second dance number. Put me down!"

When I did, she said, *"What's* over?"

"My math test," I said, still half singing. "My midterm. I hope, I hope, I hope I got a big fat B!"

"A *B?"* Cassie frowned. "Why in the world would you hope you got a B?"

That's when I remembered my lie.

We started walking to the gym, and I said, "Um, Cassie? Patti? I have something to confess. It's about the math competition."

"What?" Cassie said. "You're not in it anymore?"

"No," I said. "And I never was. I just let you jump to that conclusion. The truth is, I was basically scuba diving in math."

"Scuba diving?" asked Patti.

Cassie looked totally confused. "Tara, what are you talking about?"

"I was below C level," I said. "Get it? Anyway, I've been hanging with Kiri because she's been tutoring me. If I didn't get a B on this midterm, I'll be suspended from the squad."

"That's *awful!*" Cassie exclaimed. "Well, did you get a B?"

"I *think* so," I said as we reached the gym for our second-to-last practice. "Anyway, for right now the only numbers I have to think about are the ones in our extravaganza!"

CHAPTER
19

"*F*ive minutes to showtime," Cassie whispered. "Look out the door, Tara. The bleachers are packed! We've definitely made some money!"

I ran over and peeked out. The girls on the field hockey team were passing out programs. Inside were the words to all the cheers so everybody could cheer along. Members of the soccer team were acting as ushers, showing people where to sit. Only a few seats way at the top of the bleachers were still empty. I spotted Kiri in the first row. Boy, was *she* in for a surprise! I scanned every face in the crowd for Dad, Diane, and Lucy. I couldn't find them.

"Turn around, Tara," Mom said. Then she dabbed her long-handled brush into the blush and started dusting my cheeks. "There. That's better."

"Thanks, Mom!" I whispered.

Mom had been our costume consultant. She'd come up with some wild outfits! Mom and Eva had also volunteered to do our hair and makeup. Now the two of them were running around the girls' locker room just minutes before showtime, giving us our final dabs of blush and flicks of mascara.

"Next!" Mom called, and Patti stepped up. Not that she really needed blush to make her cheeks pink!

I peeked out the door again. Zoe Kimmel, our "lighting engineer," was sitting on a small platform above the bleachers. She was waiting for my signal. Our "sound engineer," Nash Kent, was sitting under the bleachers flipping through our tapes. Cassie had talked him into helping us hook up my boom box to the gym's sound system. Now he was waiting for Zoe's signal to start the first song.

Lauren came up behind me. "It's five, Tara," she whispered. "You ready?"

"Ready," I echoed.

Taking a deep breath, I waved to Zoe. That was it! Gradually the lights in the gym dimmed until it was almost pitch black. The crowd grew quiet. Now we had to the count of twelve to get into our formation. Nineteen girls tiptoed to the center of the gym floor. We were ready.

Bam! Zoe hit the switch for the big spot. A circle of bright white light surrounded us. It was too bright to see anybody in the bleachers. So I just had to imagine Kiri's face—and her shocked expression.

Because what that spotlight revealed wasn't listed in the program. It showed the seventh- and eighth-grade cheerleaders wearing bright blue football jerseys with yellow letters and some items we'd borrowed from the football team—helmets, shoulder pads, and pants. We were bent down, just the way football players are at the start of a game. Facing us, wearing yellow jerseys with blue letters, were the ninth-grade cheerleaders. We held this pose for thirty seconds. This was the top-secret idea Susan and Joannie had cooked up. We knew everybody in the audience was thinking the same thing: After all that fuss they're going to play powder-puff football!

Wrong!

Suddenly the spotlight spread out to light up the whole gym floor. At the same time Nash hit the Play button. Super loud rap music blasted through the gym. This was it. Showtime!

We tossed off our helmets and went into the most fantastic dance to that rap music! We boogied. We built pyramids in time to the music. We kicked in perfect synch. We spun around. We did tumbling passes that would have gotten us a first at the state competition. This was only the first number. But already the crowd was on its feet. People were cheering and clapping with the music.

The music shifted then, and we all took turns doing short little solos. Cassie and I had helped everybody choreograph their own. Patti's included a toe-touch that got everybody cheering. Cassie's had a couple of amazing ballet leaps. Lauren did a tumbling routine that about brought the house down. She finished it up with a row of back handsprings—too many to count! When my turn came all I did was dance my heart out—with a dash of shake that bootie!

When the music stopped, we ended up frozen back

in our original football player positions. We were all panting for breath. The crowd went wild, yelling and clapping and stomping like crazy. What a feeling! Nobody was ever going to call *us* powder puffs again!

Now our announcer, Beth Ann, said a few words while we dashed into the locker room. Michelle, Deesha, Isabel, and Cassie had to make a speedy costume change. Mom helped them get into bright blue long-sleeved unitards while Eva anchored bright yellow chiffon poofs to their heads with giant bobby pins. They were going right out there again to do the dance that Deesha and Michelle had choreographed. Their job was to keep the crowd pumped up while the rest of us got changed.

Those four girls didn't run out onto the floor—they cartwheeled! Nash put on a South African group playing drums, and the four whirled into their routine. It was a combination of break dancing and hip-hop. For their finale they put their arms around each other's waists and turned into the Four Rockettes! Let me tell you, those girls could *move!*

After that the four tossed away their yellow poofs. We all ran out onto the floor wearing blue unitards—looking just alike. Then we lined up for what we called the Sunny Special!

Just watch us now!
We'll show you how!
To be the best around!

That's how it started. We showed everybody how we cheered. We did double-based extensions. We popped them up, then popped them down, and right back up again. We kept every motion right on every word of that cheer. At the end we all did Herkies—just the way Patti's mom had showed us. Taking our bows, I looked out into the crowd and caught a glimpse of Mrs. Richardson's face. It brought new meaning to the word *happy!*

After that we did the number we'd done to cheer up the kids at Memorial Hospital. Then Susan took the microphone and told everyone about our squad activities. While she did that, we changed into sparkly hot-pink spandex tops and matching bike pants. Then we did our first competition cheer. The crowd went wild!

The extravaganza was incredible! It was spectacular! And it was zooming by, full speed ahead. Before I realized it, Beth Ann was announcing our finale.

"You'll notice in your program that the last number is called 'Squad Plus Three.' Let's welcome the Paxton JV cheerleaders and three guest cheerleaders!"

We all ran out onto the floor again. For this last number, we'd changed into our cheerleading uniforms. Mom and Eva had stuck little peel-off lion tatoos on our left cheeks.

Beth Ann said, "Put your hands together for three star members of the Paxton JV football team. T.D. Yeager, Drew Kelly, and Justin Dubow!"

Yes, Justin! We'd begged him and we'd pleaded. We'd coaxed and then begged some more. But finally Steve told us to cut it out. "Leave him alone," he said. "He doesn't want to."

Then—surprise! Justin had muttered, "Oh, okay, I'll do it."

Now the three boys ran out dressed in Paxton sweatsuits. They lined up with us, and we started leading a brand-new cheer—a funny one—that our whole squad had made up together. Everyone in the gym jumped up to cheer along with us:

Roar! Roar! Rah! Rah! Rah!
We're the Paxton Lions!
Roar! Rah! Rah!
We will massacre the Tigers!
We will kill the Rams and Bears!
We will slaughter every Wild Cat!
Who will stop us? No one dares!
Our teeth are sharp as razors!
We are fearless through and through!
We're the Paxton Lions but . . .
Who are you?
We're the Paxton Lions!
And we're hot, hot, hot!
Yes! We're the Paxton Lions!
And you . . . are . . . *not!*

We started it off with tumbling passes. Lauren performed a double twisting layout! We went into shoulder stands then. The boys did basket tosses first with Cassie, then Lauren, and then Michelle. As each flyer flew up into the air, she did a toe-touch! Amazing!

What a way to finish! We all lined up to take our bows. The clapping went on and on and *on.* My eyes darted from face to face in the stands. Hey! There were Dad, Diane, and Lucy! My heart did a little leap of happiness when I saw that they'd made it! But sitting right next to my dad, I saw Ms. Brickman. Now my heart sank back down. If I hadn't done well on her test, this wasn't just the end of the cheerleading extravaganza. It was the end of me as a cheerleader!

The clapping continued for so long that I decided I had to *do* something. So I ran forward and grabbed Kiri by the hand. I pulled her up into the line with us.

Then Beth Ann did something I hadn't expected. She passed me the microphone! Well, I wasn't shy. I mean, acting is in my blood! So I said, "Thank you! Thank you!" and waited until the cheering quieted down.

"Thanks for coming to our cheerleading extravaganza," I said, adding, "Make that our *first* cheerleading extravaganza."

Now everybody started clapping again!

"As I'm sure all of you know, this is Kiri Kelly. She's the editor of *Pax News*. And even though we had our little ups and downs over some of our fund-raising ideas"—I patted my cheek, and everyone started laughing—"in the end Kiri came through for us. She inspired this show, and we'd like to thank her!"

The cheerleaders clapped then along with everyone else. Over all the clapping, I whispered to Kiri, "Standing up here with us makes you an honorary cheerleader!"

"Yeah?" Kiri smiled. Then she said, "Cool."

CHAPTER
20

We did it, Tara!" Patti cried the minute we reached the girls' dressing room. "We did it!"

"We did it *right!*" Lauren added. "Did you hear all that cheering?"

"We definitely did an amazing show!" I agreed. "But did we make enough money to get us to the clinic? And did we knock Mrs. Weinstock's socks off?"

"Come on," Lauren grabbed me by the wrist and pulled me out the door. "Let's go find out."

Patti followed close behind us as we ran into the equipment room. Inside, Beth Ann had helped us set up a long table for totaling up our money. Naturally, Cassie was already there and counting.

"Hurry and count this, girls," said Beth Ann as we sat down. "Don't forget we've got a game to cheer for!" She slid a small metal box of ticket money over to each of us.

I opened the lid of mine and started counting. Seventeen twenty-dollar bills, twenty-two ten-dollar bills, twelve fives. I'd just counted a whole stack of ones when Ms. Brickman peeked in the door.

"Congratulations on your demonstration," she said, stepping into the little room. "It was very exciting."

"Thanks!" we all called back.

Then Ms. Brickman walked over to me. "Tara, you deserve double congratulations," she said.

"Oh, wow! Does that mean what I think it means?"

She nodded. "You squeaked by with a B minus on the test," she said. Then Ms. Brickman—the stone-faced Brick of all time—did something amazing. She smiled!

"Whoopie!" I shouted. "Kiri and I did it! We really did it!"

Lauren, Cassie, and Patti ran over and hugged me.

"I hope you'll keep working with Kiri," Ms. Brickman added. "By the end of the semester, you could have a solid B."

I flopped back down in my seat. What a relief! Then, back to my counting. I had to start over on the ones. I'd almost finished counting them when the door to the equipment room opened again and Mom came in.

"You were fantastic, sweetheart!" she said, throwing her arms around me.

"Thanks, Mom!" I said. "Your costumes made the extravaganza! And guess what? I got a B minus on my math test. I get to stay on the squad!"

Mom hugged me again. Just as she let go, the door opened again and in walked my Chicago family. For a minute I froze.

"Hi, Joe," Mom said. "Wasn't Tara wonderful?"

"Hi, Dottie," Dad said to Mom. "She was fantastic!"

Hey! It wasn't exactly a major reunion. But at least they'd talked to each other!

Then Mom said a quick *hi* to Diane and Lucy and slipped out the door. It made me feel awful that she left like that, all alone.

I stood up then and gave Dad a hug. "Thanks for coming," I said. I hugged Diane, too. Then I picked Lucy up.

"So Lucy-Loo," I said. "Did you like the big cheerleading extravaganza?"

Lucy squeezed me around the neck. I took that for a *yes!*

"It was just wonderful, Tara," Diane said. "You are one incredible dancer! We're so proud of you!"

"We are," said Dad. "I wouldn't have missed this for the world." He held up his video camera. "And I've got the whole thing on tape."

Hey! Move over, Lucy, baby! I thought. *Your big sis is getting some tape time for herself!*

Lots of people found their way into the equipment room to congratulate us after that. Patti's mom and dad and Missy came in. So did Lauren's brother, Jed, and Salleen. Cassie's dad showed up. He said he'd videotaped the whole show, too.

Just when I thought not one more person could fit into that tiny room, Mrs. Weinstock walked in.

"Congratulations, girls!" she said. "Every cheer you did was a showstopper."

"Thanks!" we all called.

"I'd just like to say," she went on, "that as a member

134

of the school finance committee, I'll certainly do what I can to get the cheerleader budget increased."

"All right!" we called out.

Mrs. Weinstock talked to Beth Ann for a few minutes then. Just before she headed for the door, I *thought* I heard her say, "Cheerleading has really changed since I was on my high school squad."

Finally Beth Ann had to shoosh everybody out. Then we got down to serious counting. When I finally totaled up the cash in my box, it came to $695. Cassie added that to the total of all the boxes we'd been counting.

"Okay," she called. "Our grand total is . . . drumroll, please . . ."

We all started thumping our hands on the table in imitation of a drumroll.

". . . is two thousand, six hundred fifty-five dollars."

"That's almost three thousand dollars!" I shouted.

"It's close," Cassie agreed. "We can definitely send in our deposit by the deadline." She hit a few buttons on her calculator. "That means we just need to make $345 before spring break."

"Hey," I said, "I know how we can do it!"

No one said a word. They all just looked at me, horrified.

"Don't get nervous," I told them. "I'm all out of showbiz ideas. What I was going to suggest was a car wash or a raffle or a bake sale—something that's really, really easy and really, really *boring!*"

About the Author

KATY HALL grew up outside of St. Louis, Missouri, where she rooted for the Ladue High Rams. She has written four novels for middle-grade readers and has collaborated with Lisa Eisenberg on more than twenty humor books for young readers, including *Batty Riddles* (Dial) and *The Family Survival Handbook* (Scholastic). Ms. Hall lives in New York City with her husband, daughter, and two cats, and enjoys attending plays and ballet performances.

Can superpowers be super-cool?

Meet Alex Mack. It's her first day of junior high and *everything* goes wrong! Until an accident leaves her with special powers. . .powers that can be hard to control. It's exciting. . .and a little scary!

ALEX, YOU'RE GLOWING!

by Diana G. Gallagher

Available in mid-March 1995

A new title every other month!

Based on the hit series from Nickelodeon®

 A MINSTREL® BOOK

Published by Pocket Books